IMPOSSIBLE MUSIC

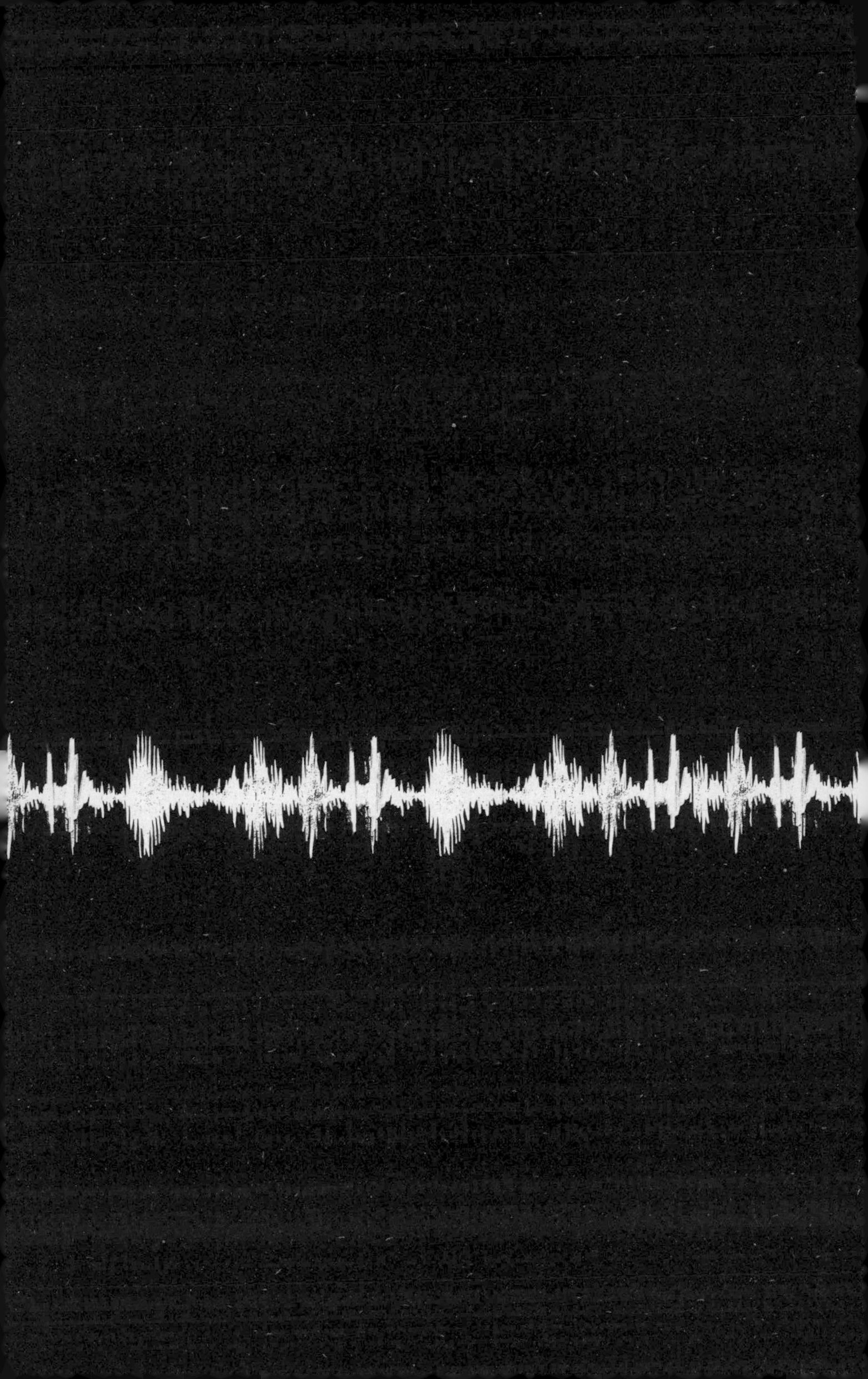

IMPOSSIBLE MUSIC

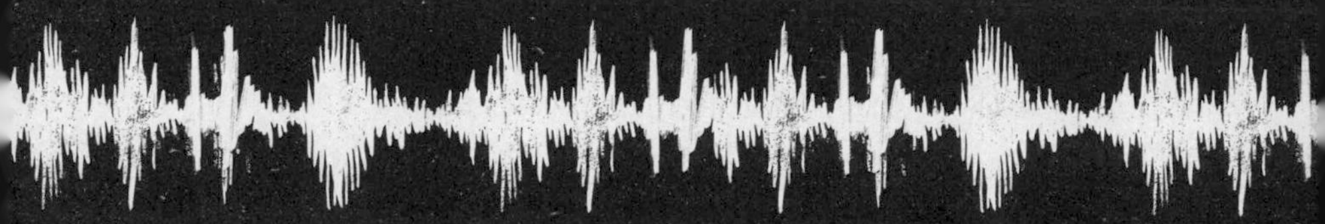

SEAN WILLIAMS

CLARION BOOKS
Houghton Mifflin Harcourt
Boston New York

This project has been assisted by the Australian Government through
the Australia Council, its arts funding and advisory body,
and the Government of South Australia through Arts SA.

Government of South Australia

Arts South Australia

Clarion Books
3 Park Avenue
New York, New York 10016

Clarion Books is an imprint of Houghton Mifflin Harcourt Publishing Company.

hmhbooks.com

The text was set in Sabon MT Std.

Library of Congress Cataloging-in-Publication Data
Names: Williams, Sean, author.
Title: Impossible Music / Sean Williams.
Description: Boston; New York : Clarion Books, Houghton Mifflin Harcourt,
[2019] | Summary: In a class for the newly deaf, former musician Simon meets G and his
quest to create an entirely new form of music helps him better understand her, himself,
and his relationship to the hearing world.
Identifiers: LCCN 2018051216 | ISBN 9780544816206 (hardcover)
Subjects: | Deaf—Fiction. | People with disabilities—Fiction. | Musicians—Fiction. |
Dating (Social customs)—Fiction.
Classification: PZ7.W6681739 Imp 2019 | DDC [E]—dc23
LC record available at https://lccn.loc.gov/2018051216

Printed in the United States of America
DOC 10 9 8 7 6 5 4 3 2 1
4500758182

For my sister, Christyna,
and Rachel, my sister in crime

The sign language in this novel is Auslan,
the language of the Australian Deaf community.
I have taken some liberties with regional variants.

"Perhaps music happens elsewhere than in ears."

Anna Smaill, *The Chimes*

INTRO

HEATHLAND GURU

December 21

How?

"Small word, big question." That's what Mum used to say when too tired to answer properly. Only it's not a small word anymore, not for me.

"How?" in Australian sign language, a.k.a. Auslan, starts with two palms held upward, one above the other. You slide your hands apart to create a space between them, and they stay facing up, empty—the idea being, I guess, for someone to metaphorically fill them with knowledge. I think of it as a shrugless *huh?*

It's a big sign, then, rather than a small word, but the question remains huge.

I think G knows that, which is why it's taken her so long to ask.

We're sitting side by side in a corner of the campus that most people avoid because it's too noisy. Perhaps that's what drew us here. The first time I came to the University of Adelaide—

for a winter school held in the holidays between second and third terms, when everyone else was heading northward for warmth—the renovations were annoying, but I can't hear them now. All I can feel is the occasional vibration as machines hammer and thunder on the other side of a canvas fence, invisible but present—like our uncertain futures. Everything has been thoroughly overturned in the last three months and nineteen days.

G has her knees drawn up tight to her chest, scuffed Doc Martens jammed hard on the bench as though she's bracing herself to jump. When she's not talking, her hands clutch her forearms in a monkey grip, scars vivid violet like they've been drawn on with marker. We're so close our hips are touching, and I consciously note for the first time that she doesn't smell like other girls. Where most I know are too sharp and sweet, she's pleasantly sour, lemon in hot tea. With every breath, I strain to take in a bit more of her.

We've been seeing a lot of each other lately, but I've not yet admitted to myself that I'm falling in love with her. This is just one of many things I can't put into words. How can I? All I have are numb approximations—shapes in the air that bear no relation at all to sound or language or music, as irrelevant as my fingers on the neck of my guitar . . .

G nudges me with her shoulder, reminding me of the question, and I nod, reaching into my pocket. Some things are easier to explain by phone, or at least less impossible.

I have brain damage.

She, leaning closer to read the words on my phone's glowing screen, makes a gesture I guess means, *Tell me something I don't already know.* I scrunch up the left side of my face and keep tapping on the screen.

No, really. Bilateral embolic stroke to Heschl's gyrus.

I haven't typed the words to anyone before, so the phone autocorrects the last two to "Heathland Guru." It sounds like a band but not a good one, a bland purveyor of the kind of Top 40 shit that I once loved to hate but now would kill to hear.

Ears work fine, but my brain is deaf as a post.

G snatches the phone from me and types: Hysterical?

I think she's being ironic before I absorb the question mark. Trying not to bristle, I answer, I'm not imagining it. I can show you the scans if you want.

She reaches behind me and puts her hand on my neck, thumb and fingers on either side of my spine, and butts my shoulder with her right temple. The smell of her becomes much stronger. I tilt my head and breathe in deeply, clearing my mental sinuses: hair, skin, G. Maybe I'm smelling a bit of her home as well, and suddenly I really want to see where she eats, where she watches TV, where she sleeps.

While I'm lost in a pleasantly detailed daydream, she takes the phone and types something with her left hand.

Well, thanks to you and your gimpy gyrus, I've lost a bet.

It's my turn to make the ***how?*** sign, which creates a small space between us. Her hand leaves my neck. She sits straight as she taps out the words.

Rock god goes deaf, duh. You didn't say, so we thought you were embarrassed about blowing your eardrums out onstage. As you should have been. So obvious—

I snatch the phone from her.

You think I'm that stupid?

I don't mention the times I gigged without plugs or practiced solos with my headphones turned up so loud my ears rang for hours.

She snatches the phone back.

Being deaf is . . .

She stops Swyping, and I stare at those three words, knowing she was about to write *stupid* but thought better of it. There's no reason to make it personal.

At the same time, though, her auditory nerves aren't going to magically repair themselves any more than my Heschl's gyrus is going to hatch like a cocoon to reveal a beautiful butterfly. When we're angry, we have to blame something.

Or change the subject.

How much did you lose on the bet?

A round of drinks for the whole class.

When did all this happen?

One of the many days you didn't show.

I'm not pissed at G, but it does shit me a little that she and the rest of the newly deaf discussed me behind my back.

Farid said you showed all the signs of traumatic brain injury. Everyone agreed.

Except you.

Don't give me a medal or anything. I thought you were an idiot for playing your amp too loud.

She's smiling. I can see her expression reflected in the strengthened glass.

I need to do something to regain the initiative. Can't have her thinking I'm the punch line of a bad joke.

You ever hear any Blackmod?

That was the name of my last band. I am briefly but immensely relieved it wasn't one of the others: Ratzinger, InTerrorBang, übertor, Anal Twin . . .

She signs, *No*.

I stand up and strike a pose: imaginary guitar in left hand, pick held high in right, hair swept over my shoulder, grimace. Never forget the grimace. With the sound of remembered drums in my useless ears, I bring my right hand down for the opening chord of "Intoxicated Tyrants." The moves are fresh in my mind, having played through it only yesterday, on a real instrument, for the benefit of no one but myself. This time, I rapid-fire air-guitar and head-bang for G in our secluded corner of the campus, playing in time to the hammering from the science wing, mouthing the growls and sneering the squeals of my former bandmates' lyrics, and wishing with all my heart that it was more than just a fantasy, this gift I'm giving her. This piece of me that I cling to, even though everyone tells me it is dead. Hell, my parents and counselors even held a *funeral* for it . . .

Hair sways across my face like a curtain, sticking to my heat-dampened skin. I couldn't look at her if I wanted, but I wouldn't anyway until I'm finished. Her laughter will put me off my stride, and I need this mad rain dance to my treacherous brain cells just as much as she needs to understand that I would never, ever have seriously put my hearing at risk.

Only when I have thrashed my way through the final syncopated cadence do I flick the hair out of my eyes and realize that she is crying.

Triumph turns to shock. Dropping my pose along with the imaginary guitar, I kneel in front of her and take her hands in mine, mouthing words neither of us can hear. *What's wrong?*

There's a message already typed into the phone.

That's how it sounds in my head.

Fast.

Busy.

Loud.

I could kick myself. She leans forward and butts my shoulder again, only this time it is me cupping her neck where shaved hairline meets naked skin. There's another scar there, thin and fresh, one I've never noticed before. Now's not the time to ask. I am still sweating from my performance, and I hope that doesn't make her feel worse than I already have. But I suppose if it did she would pull away or push me off or somehow make her feelings clear. She's much better at that than I am.

Instead I'm the one who pulls away, taking the phone and typing:

Tinnitus is . . .

I stop there, because I can't say *stupid* any more than G could.

I also can't say: *And if you didn't have it, we would never have met.*

PART ONE

"THE DRAPERY FALLS"

September 2

The last words I ever heard were my mother telling me to turn my music off and go to sleep, it being a Wednesday and she having to work early the next day. Mum crunches numbers in an office for a living. Statistics and other things I don't understand, although I like that she has in her head a seemingly inexhaustible supply of facts and figures, such as the odds of dying from a drug overdose (1/13,333) or the number of places in Australia named after Queen Victoria (21). She scatters them like punctuation marks across nights when my sister and I are home, probably because they're more likely to get a reaction than the things she'd rather tell us, such as number of children (2), amount of love (infinite).

"Turn your music off, honey. It's a school night."

Headphones were invented for utterly unreasonable requests like this, so after Mum stuck her head around my door, I stayed up an hour or two, chatting with friends online and listening to —I regret this now—the latest from a band called Electric Sky

Prawn. If I'd known that *Sproutrider* would be the last album I'd ever hear, I would've picked something better. *Blackwater Park*, perhaps. Go into silence with the slow fadeout of "The Drapery Falls" still ringing in my ears—that's what I would choose now.

The idea of choice, though, is as much a fantasy as that ancient ethical fake-out: *Which would you rather be, deaf or blind?* No one can possibly answer that question. No one should ever have to answer that question. It's meaningless, existing only as a reminder to treat what we have with reverence, I guess.

The last sound I ever heard might have been the click of my light switch or the rustle of the pillow case as I rolled over. Our neighbor's dog barking at a cat? One final late-night fart? I don't remember. Because I didn't know I *needed* to remember.

That September, in my former life, I thought all sound was music. I took it for granted, paid so little attention to the symphony surrounding me that I missed its ending.

Cases of cortical deafness in the history of medicine? Twelve, one for every note of the chromatic scale.

I am the thirteenth.

Medical specialists explained it to me afterwards as best they could, given that I couldn't hear a word they were saying. My eyes scanned the documents they'd printed out, dense paragraphs forming a wagon train around the tiny blood vessel that had burst during my sleep, drowning that critical part of my brain. Really, though, my attention was on Mum. She was listening closely to those specialists, whose mouths were making silent glyphs I utterly failed to interpret. Selwyn Floyd, with his ridiculous goatee that looked like he'd dyed it in milk. His younger sidekick, Prameela Verma, mostly speechless for now. I had learned to read Mum's body language much better in recent days. As she listened, she crushed in on herself like a car in an accident with a semi.

The message had finally gotten through, which was ironic: Mum could hear the words better than I could. She just didn't want to listen.

I didn't need ears to understand what she had been told, or to recognize how it made her feel.

It was a struggle, however, to feel anything at all around the absence, the ghastly void where every sound in the world had once been. The bickering of birds. The rumble of distant traffic. The hiss of springtime rain. It was like I'd woken up that fateful day with my head in a bucket of water, but a thousand times worse. I felt drowned by nothing, smothered by silence. I kept putting my fingers to my ears as though I could remove the obstacle between me and the hearing world, but there was no obstacle there, of course. The problem wasn't on the outside.

Later I would scream and scream in vain, trying to hear something—my own anguish, at the very least. Anything. But all I got for my efforts was a raw throat.

Deafness, I learned fast, is not just the absence of noise. It is not being in a cave or an old mine or a soundproofed room. Deafness is the eradication of the possibility of noise, including the pulsing heart, the bellowing lungs, the soft hiss of blood through vessels near the ear—all that previously unnoticed body language, stopped forever.

People are musical instruments, just like my guitar, but we learn from long habit to tune out our personal symphony. We only notice it when it's going wrong—or gone completely, when the symphony is over and the orchestra has left the stage.

DIVA HAMMER

December 3

Her name isn't really G. It's George. Not Georgie or Georgina —she made that very clear in our first class together, three weeks after I lost my hearing—but no one deaf cares about those extra syllables, or the name her parents gave her, for that matter. They're just mouth shapes. She, like the rest of us, needed a new name, one given by someone from the community they told us we now belonged to.

Her deaf name comes from the sign for the letter *G*—right fist on top of left fist—with an added circular twist evoking her love of caffeine (it looks a bit like someone strangling a chicken). For a while she signed off her messages as *George-who-loves-coffee,* while she got used to the idea.

Deaf names are given, but they're not always wanted.

That was how we first got to know each other, via Messenger. It was too hard to talk in deaf class, concentrating as we were on reluctantly learning the bare minimum to get by. ***Hello. How much? Help!*** If we were paired together to practice what we learned that day, she made it clear she was as unwilling a participant as me. Her hands hung at her sides until she was forced to speak. When she did, her signs would be cursory and hard to read, or so exaggerated when I failed to understand her that they became almost aggressive, chopping and wrenching at the air. I thought her issue was with me, something I had unknowingly done. After all, it couldn't have been anything I said. Only later, when a message from *George-who-loves-coffee* arrived out of the blue, did I realize that she wasn't angry at me. Just at being unable to hear.

Still, I was cautious. Perhaps too cautious. More than two months into the online conversation, she asked if I'd like to go see a roller derby bout with her. I wasn't sure if it was a date and was too nervous to ask straight up, but I said yes, from loneliness and at least partly out of interest.

It was impossible not to be curious. Her fringe was pink back then, bright and in-your-face, not at all like she smells. She wore straightforward black tights and untucked white shirts, occasionally black jeans and suspenders, if she was meeting friends afterwards. (That stopped pretty quickly. Maintaining hearing friendships is hard work for both sides.) On the inside of her right forearm is a tattoo of a skull. Later, beneath it, she would add the word *Deaf* in bold Gothic script, daring people to think it a typo. Her square face and broad jaw with a surprisingly small mouth makes her look at times like a young Helena Bonham Carter—not my type at all, I would once have said. I always went for skinny girls in tight jeans, the kind who thought being with a too-tall, long-haired guitarist was a good look. G is nothing like them. Her ears have never once been pierced, an idiosyncrasy she maintains as though it's some kind of revolutionary distinction. Me, I have enough metal in my ears for both of us.

When you're talking in sign, you're supposed to focus on someone's face rather than what the rest of them is doing, but that's hard for beginners. On those few occasions our Auslan teacher did manage to coax us into hesitant conversation (***Is there a bus stop near here? I really want to know. Why is this so difficult?***), I found myself staring at her hands rather than what she was saying. (*No. So? Because!*) Her fingers were short and tapering, her nails tidy and unpolished, her palms unexpectedly narrow with wrists to match. The scars were what I couldn't take my eyes off, once I noticed them. Waxy and lumpy, like a wrestler's ear, they weren't the work of a cutter—too public, too thick—and they didn't look like a suicide attempt, either. They were so thick she would've bled out in seconds. I was curious to know their origins but never got around to finding the right way to ask, and she didn't volunteer anything, at first.

Instead, over Messenger, we chatted about usual stuff. Our families (struggling to deal with our new way of being), the shitty lag of closed-captioning on TV (no one likes being last in the room to get the joke), what we were thinking about taking at university next year. She had applied to study social work, while I had intended to pursue a degree in music performance at Adelaide Uni. I was still playing guitar solos at night while everyone slept, and playing well, inasmuch as I could tell, but the question of whether I would be allowed to study music at all was still horribly open. Nowhere in the fine print did the uni say that hearing was a prerequisite, but it had to be, surely?

Small talk, in other words, albeit revealing. I was pleased I hadn't done anything specific to piss G off but understood that it remained a possibility. She was prickly, ending conversations without warning or making sharp remarks that I wasn't entirely sure were entirely jokes.

I didn't learn the source of her enigmatic scars until the roller derby maybe-date, the first time we used our phones to talk to each other face-to-face. (Sign language gave me a headache when I stuck at it too long, plus we were aware of whole vocabularies we hadn't learned yet. The only thing we'd become truly proficient at was swearing.) I wore a T-shirt for a band called The Ubiquitous Pig, and Stanley, their starred-and-striped mascot, looked right at home next to G's animated rockabilly look. She had dyed her hair purple and wore sky-blue lipstick.

Here's our first proper conversation, transcribed by my phone's voice recognition system and saved for posterity. I've added punctuation and fixed typos because the raw file is all **this is cheating** why we have the technology **that doesn't mean its right**, and no one wants to read that.

She asked, You ever seen a bout before?

No. You?

Heaps. My team's on tonight. We were junior champs three years in a row.

You skated?

Hell yes. I was the jammer.

The what?

Simon, Simon, Simon. Tell me, why did I bring you again?

So you can show off, I'm guessing. Which team was yours?

The Doom Kitteh Brawlers.

Wow, my phone did not like that.

Wait until it hears my derby name: Arya Ghostclown.

Seriously?

AKA the Diva Hammer.

L.

What?

That's LOL without the OL.

See my face? That's LOL without the OL or the L.

I bet you were a mean skater.

The meanest and the best.

Can you still do it since you-know-what?

Sure, but I fell last year and broke my wrists. Had to have reconstructive surgery. You noticed the scars, right? Everyone does.

Yes. And ouch.

The pain was the easy part. Imagine trying to wipe your bum with both hands in plaster.

TMI!

Wait till I start flirting.

Yay?

Anyway, my hands are okay now, and I've still got my strength. Could skate if I wanted to. Totally. Be like getting on a bike—but if I ever fall on my hands again, how do I talk? What happens when our voices change? I don't think Siri has a language setting for deaf as fuck.

Doesn't matter what your voice sounds like to me. It's the best voice I never heard.

Now who's flirting?

I was a bit, but mainly I was trying to change the subject. I knew all about the "deaf voice." My sister, Maeve, loved to tell me when I was talking too quietly or too loudly, and that wasn't the worst of it. People who can't hear themselves talk steadily lose all the subtlety of intonation that hearing people are used to. One day, I knew, my voice would be flat and monotonous, perhaps even unpleasantly robotic to listen to, and that worried me more than I liked to admit. I could only avoid it by using my guitar tuner to check my pitch—and Maeve would get a real kick out of that.

The skate derby provided a welcome distraction on a highly visceral level. I could *feel* the crowd like a herd of wild creatures stampeding all around me. I kept my hands flat on the chair beside my thighs, relishing the vibrations of the skaters as they went by, the crunch of collisions between flesh and bone and the thud of impacts on the track. Maybe I was fooling myself, but it seemed as though I could actually differentiate each class of sound. It was like being at a gig, searching for the lead and vocals through the mud of bass and drums. Searching and failing, usually.

The Doom Kitteh Brawlers won decisively and bloodily, with the majority of injuries accrued by the opposing team. G stood and clapped like a hearing person, and her mouth opened and closed in what I assumed were shouts of delight and encouragement. No one could tell that she was different. I could see why she liked that.

On the way back to my car, she asked me, So what do you do for kicks when you're not watching girls in skates beat each other up?

Play guitar, I told her.

But you can't hear it.

So? I still like to play. Not being able to hear didn't stop Beethoven playing the piano.

You think you're as good as Beethoven?

Maybe just as pig-headed. If he didn't give up, why should I?

G laughed with her eyes and her lips like I'd never seen her laugh before. She was beautiful in an entirely new way, and I was glad when she put her phone in her pocket in order to take my hand. I smiled at her as we walked through a tunnel of silence, feeling genuinely happy for the first time in a long while. We'd spent the night cheating on Auslan by using dictation apps, but this was real. This was real communication.

THE BROWN NOTE

September 2

My high school music teacher was a short, round, bald man called Ian Mackereth. Stick him in a wig and fake beard and he'd look at home in *The Hobbit,* but with an acoustic guitar in his hands he becomes a true wizard. He can play anything—and I mean *anything*. Folk, classical, rock, metal, jazz . . . His ear is so good you can play him a track once and he'll be able to reproduce it afterwards. The important bits, anyway. He can do this, he told me way back when, because he studied theory as well as practice: he can sense what's under the surface of the music, which makes recreating the bits most people notice that much easier. The waves tripping over submerged mountains, where the waves are melody and the theory is that which lies beneath.

I wasn't so sure about this at school. All I wanted to do was ape my favorite solos. But I guess some of his lessons sank in because I aced the midyear exams he'd helped me prepare for, and suddenly the thought of studying music at university didn't seem so unlikely. I had always wanted to play guitar after high school. With a degree, I could teach if my rock god career failed to deliver.

I found out later that Mr. Mackereth moonlighted as a busker, something my school frowned upon. He went up in my estimation a notch right then. Screw the alma mater. You could be short, round, and bald, and still kick some kind of ass.

Also, it amused me to walk past him playing flamenco Beatles covers in Rundle Mall, collecting gold coins in the hat at his feet. Rock on, Mr. Mackereth, you sellout.

Professor Dorn, who taught the seven-day winter school I attended at Adelaide Uni, could not be more different. Grace Dorn is a tall, stiff-backed woman who wears her white hair super short, barely there at all. I can't say I warmed to her immediately: everything in her tone betrayed that she had better things to do than talk to a bunch of students who didn't know a sus2 from a sostenuto.

She also teaches an advanced composition program for students handpicked from each year's applicants, and I guess the winter school is a way of meeting some of these applicants ahead of their exams. It became clear over the winter school week that she and I shared an interest in music that went deeper than notes and theory. A *philosophical* kinship, if you like. Already I was of the opinion that the click and hum you heard when you plugged your guitar into an amp was as valid a musical statement as the opening notes of the song you went on to play. *There's no such thing as unmusical sound,* I liked to say, and except for when Maeve played her crappy music too loud, I even meant it.

Professor Dorn touched lightly on noise music during one winter school class. Afterwards, I asked her about it. She suggested I read some of John Cage's lectures on the relationship between music and noise—which were mind-blowing—and listen to other pioneering noise composers on YouTube. I did everything she said and then looked up her own compositions online. One called "The Grand Kenotaphion" consisted of all the two-minute silences held on Remembrance Sunday, as recorded by the BBC over a century-plus, mashed together into something that is very far from silence, a melange of crowd noises, radio announcers, birds, and the echoes of bells dispersing out across the crowd.

Silence as noise . . . I loved it as a concept, never for a moment imagining that one day I would grapple with it for real.

If there is such thing as an unmusical sound, it would surely be the legendary brown note, a tone pitched very, very low, at exactly the right frequency to relax the bowels of anyone exposed to it. Boom: they instantly shit themselves. Some people deny that the brown note exists. Dad thinks the military is just itching for the chance to test it on protestors.

That first day in Selwyn Floyd's office, reading the words the specialists had typed out for me, I felt as though someone had hit me with the brown note, volume turned right up to eleven.

. . . extremely rare form of sensorineural hearing loss . . . inability to perceive words, music, or environmental sounds . . . no apparent injury to the inner ear function . . . brainstem auditory responses normal, but cortical evoked potentials appear impaired . . .

"You can fix this, right?"

Everyone in the room stopped talking and turned to look at me. They could hear me perfectly well, even if I couldn't hear myself or them. The sound of my voice seemed to shut them up, as though they'd forgotten I was there—written me off as deaf, disabled, absent, gone. Nonparticipant in the conversation and therefore nonparticipant in life. Reminding them that I existed silenced them for real.

I saw a look of something that might have been shame cross Prameela's face as Selwyn reached for a notepad and began to scribble.

"Right?" I repeated.

Mum's face crumpled, and suddenly she was holding me, pressing me to her, her hands wrapped tightly around my head, as though she could possibly protect me from a harm that had already occurred.

Through that tangle of maternal limbs came Selwyn's note. Scrawled in barely decipherable doctor's script, he had written:

We'll do everything we can.

I wanted to say, *Don't bullshit me, I can take it.* But I wasn't sure I *could* take it. And he wasn't bullshitting, not really.

The mind is a complex and plastic thing, he explained to me via a subsequent series of notes. Sometimes people recover from strokes so well you'd never know they'd been injured at all. Undamaged parts of the brain take over from where the dead parts leave off, like runners in a relay or the pianists in Erik Satie's marathon eighteen-hour work *Vexations*. Given time, Selwyn was thinking, I might completely recover.

He had hope. Therefore, I should have hope too. It was allowed. Perhaps, I told myself, it wouldn't matter if I lost a few notes of my personal symphony if I could pick it up again later.

Perhaps this brief interlude of silence could even be part of it. A rest that had already lasted entirely too long for my liking.

How it happened (returning to G's big question, because there's absolutely no small answer) is that I woke up and couldn't hear. I didn't know that I had suffered a stroke while I slept. I had no headache, misbehaving pupils, or malfunctioning limbs. Neither had I lost the ability to speak, although that was difficult to tell at the time because, well, the obvious.

This was in September, two months after winter school and Professor Dorn and John Cage. My first thought was nothing profound: *It's so quiet.* Meaning the house, not the inside of my head. It was dark, as well. My phone said 4:03 a.m. Something must have woken me, but what? Maybe Maeve sneaking back in after an unusually late midnight smoke. Maybe the neighbor's dog. Maybe nothing. The nothing of silence.

Silence has pressure and weight. It grinds you down, and I suppose that could have been what woke me. As my inability to hear unusual sounds was matched by an equally strange inability to hear *usual* sounds, I woke up a bit more and sleepily stuck my fingers in my ears, thinking I'd fallen asleep with my headphones in, or maybe my auditory canals had gotten stopped up with an improbable amount of wax. All felt normal in there . . . except that I couldn't hear the scrape and swirl of my probing finger.

I said something—*That's fucking weird,* or words to that effect—and I couldn't hear this either. The silence was complete. All sound had fled.

By that time, I was wide awake, sitting upright in bed with the light on and crushing a pillow with both hands into my lap. My heart was pounding—I could feel it but not hear it—and the desperate thought, *This has to be a nightmare,* was on a loop in my mind. I detected no sign of waking up, though. What happened next? How did I make it end?

At some point I must have called for Mum because I remember her bursting into the room, mouth forming shapes that might have meant "what's wrong?" or "what's going on?" or "where's Obi-Wan?" for all I could tell. She was as noiseless as her footsteps and the door handle.

The fright she gave me when she appeared only compounded my growing panic.

"I can't hear," I told her. "I can't hear!"

I must've shouted more loudly than I intended to. Next, Maeve was in my room, looking annoyed in her Taylor Swift squirrel pajamas and at the same time curious to know why I was the one causing a late-night fuss for a change. Curiosity turned to concern as Mum enlisted her in testing the boundaries of my symptoms: clapping hands, clicking fingers, yelling. None of their attempts elicited a flicker of a response. It was as though my ears had suddenly turned off.

Mum found a pen and some paper—not easy in the tangled web of cables, guitars, and amps in my room—and wrote me a note. It said:

Get dressed. I'll take you to the hospital. Don't worry. We'll fix it, promise. XX

JUDD NELSON OVERDRIVE

December 10

There was an upside to not being able to talk to each other like G and I might have if we'd met, well, *before*. How to tell a girl that sports never interested me much, on roller skates or otherwise? Better not to try, I decided, this early in a potential relationship, because it could make people regard you skeptically, like saying you didn't like kids or kittens.

Nothing against sports personally. It's just that I didn't get it when I was a kid, and now I'm too far behind to catch up. When I'm dragged along by my mates, I find myself swept up in a thing that's bigger than me, a thing that has its own opinions on what will happen at any random moment. It's disconcerting.

Not hearing makes that feeling worse. It's harder to sense the mood of a crowd if you can't hear it. A crowd is just a bunch of people opening and closing their mouths and waving their arms in the air. Unless you have someone explaining it to you.

People who don't like music must feel the same way about concerts.

The knowledge that I had different tastes from a lot of my

friends didn't sink in until I learned to play music. My dad was the one who got me started. I was twelve and came home from school to find a guitar leaning against my bed, a Post-it note stuck to it saying *Happy belated birthday*. Dad had dropped it off that day, with Mum's permission. Things were tense between them then. He was only allowed in the house while she was there and we weren't. I didn't know that until Maeve told me much later. Maeve is younger than me, but not by much, and despite their constant bickering, shares more with Mum than I'll ever know about, hopefully.

The guitar was a cheap Yamaha acoustic, the standard model that music students have been learning on for generations. I'd seen them in school, and I knew in principle how to hold one.

Alone in my room, I sat on my bed and took up the instrument. It was surprisingly light in my arms. I'd never realized that guitars were hollow, like a held breath.

I selected a string at random. Plucked it. And suddenly this inanimate lump of wood became extraordinary.

It vibrated. It resonated. It sang.

The note surrounded me like a giant bubble, and I fell into it, as though the floor of my room had dropped away. I was weightless, entering a realm where the usual physics no longer applied. That bubble felt like home, a place where I was safe and surrounded by wonders.

Every note I've played since has been a step deeper into

Narnia or Middle Earth, en route to the Magical North where all bets are off.

Until the bubble popped and all the music left the world.

Take me to a concert, G said in a message, three months and seven days after I lost my hearing. You owe me.

Owe you what?

A night out. An experience. A reason to get out of bed this weekend. Take your pick.

It wasn't a big ask. I already had an invite-plus-one for a show that weekend. Judd Nelson Overdrive was a melodic death metal band from Canberra I'd been wanting to see for years, and I wasn't going to let a small thing like not being able to hear stop me.

When I told G about the gig, she said, Sure, and I said, Great, and thus it was settled. Or so I thought.

We had kissed a little after the roller derby bout but hadn't seen each other since, because I was no longer going to deaf class. This sounded like second date material to me, or another audition. I could tell that she was testing me. And why not? Kissing in complete silence is weird at first, like doing it for the first time all over again, and so is getting to know someone without hearing them speak.

Taking G to a concert was something of a test on my part too, to be completely honest. I've been seeing live music at underage gigs since I was thirteen, and first played at the Jade

Monkey when I was fourteen and a half. The shows I go to are so loud you can feel the sound hitting you like a physical force—which is exactly what sound is, on a molecular level. Pressure waves expand and compress across our bodies, and inside our bodies too if the noise is big enough. The first time I went right up close to the speakers, I thrilled at the waves of focused energy literally pouring through me. When I stood at the back, the muddled wash of echoes I absorbed made me feel as though I was floating in a gentle surf. In general, I prefer to be in the thick of it, being pummeled by people rather than pressure waves.

Gigs like this are a great leveler. Above a certain volume, we're all deaf.

It'd been a crappy week, thanks to a certain newspaper article and the three-month anniversary of my stroke, but it was looking up now. If G liked the concert, that would make it even better.

She and I arranged to meet a couple of blocks away in order to negotiate the door bitch together. People there knew I was deaf. Some even knew my new name: left hand raised in a fist except for a crooked little finger (half an *S*) combined with right hand strumming an imaginary guitar. I was keen to spare G the hassle of passing notes back and forth just to get inside.

Five minutes before she was due, she sent me a text saying,

Sorry. It's not going to work tonight.

I tried not to be disappointed.

What's wrong? Everything okay?

She didn't reply until I was inside and the gig had started, and the buzz of my phone went unnoticed through the assault of the concert. I felt bad later, but what could I do? Phones solve just one communications bottleneck. You can't make a deaf person talk if they won't look at you or respond to your texts. And you can't wait around forever.

The concert was good. Fast, busy, loud. My ears felt it deep in their fragile bones, even though my brain no longer knew what it was supposed to be. Every other part of a gig—the smell of sweat, the taste of beer, the flashing of lights, the close proximity of people in the mosh pit—was present and correct, vital and reviving, going some way to filling the yawning chasm at the center of my existence. *What is the sound of music,* I told myself, *but just the most obvious part?*

As I came out of the club, I quickly waved good night and peeled away from the safe crowd of my friends to avoid the awkwardness that inevitably descended when normal speaking rules resumed.

Only then did I notice the texts G had sent.

Imagine your least favorite song.

Imagine your least favorite bit of your least favorite song.

Now, imagine that bit stuck on a loop, and nothing you do can shake it. It goes around and around, the same few notes, over and over, unchanging, like it's never going to end. Not until you're completely fucking crazy.

I have that tonight.

The earworm from hell.

That's why I didn't come to the concert. It's not you, it's the music. Sorry.

Still feeling a bit of a beer buzz, I refused to take that as a blanket rejection of everything I held dear.

Two words for you: Good Vibrations.

Her reply was instantaneous: Are you kidding me?

Never Gonna Give You Up.

You bastard.

The Macarena.

Stop!

. . . In the Name of Love? . . . Hammer Time?

She was silent for a while after that, long enough to suggest that maybe I'd been insensitive, joking about something that was obviously a big deal to her. I didn't really know what tinnitus was like, although of course I'd read about it since meeting her. Tinnitus isn't deafness per se: instead of the ears' wiring not working, the wiring detects sounds where there are none. Phantom noises, like phantom limbs, can be irritating, even frightening—and they can drown out all other sounds if they're loud enough, making someone *effectively* deaf, like G . . . but could these noises really be musical? If G was describing a literal thing in her head right now, then yes, and it sounded like a fucking nightmare, maybe one I had carelessly made much worse.

But hell, a tiny part of me said in response, *she's still got* music.

Home was a half-hour walk away—the journey had never spooked me until I was unable to hear the sound of people creeping up on me. No one ever did, but that didn't stop me from looking around every few seconds, just in case.

Halfway there, my phone buzzed.

Are you flirting again? (Say yes.)

Yes. (Why?)

Good. (Because it's distracting.)

We could take it to the next level. (We *should* take it to the next level.)

Which is? (How many levels are there? (Typing in brackets is a pain in the arse!))

What part of "Hammer Time" was unclear? (Let's find out. (Agreed. (But why stop now?)))

I am pulling my "That's so not happening tonight" face. (But thank you for giving me something else to think about. (Seriously. (Maybe next time. (Good night.))))

With that she was gone, and I trudged on alone, feeling the crunch of the pavement under my feet and a cool breeze across my forehead. I made the sign for her name, the *G* with a twist, and admired the "sound" of it. I liked the "feel" of "George." I liked the sound of *Maybe next time* even better.

GHOST SPRAY

September 7

Any kid who has a wardrobe in their room goes through a phase of being afraid of it. Mine is a hulking old heirloom, dark and brooding, with a wood grain pattern that looks like a hooded person standing with their face in permanent shadow. When shifting light hits it through my half-open door, as someone walks up the hallway, say, the figure seems to turn and look at me with cruel fingers unfurling . . .

God, the sleepless nights that thing has caused!

So convinced was I that the figure in the wardrobe was *literally* going to kill me, snatch me up into its dusty depths the *very moment* my eyelids closed, that Mum resorted to desperate measures to get me to stay in bed. Ghost Spray, she told me, was the world's most powerful deterrent against all things supernatural. Just one squirt could dispel not just ghosts, but also goblins, ghouls, and any other gremlins waiting to get me. Since I was so upset, she'd give the wardrobe *three* squirts. All right, five—to be *absolutely* sure.

I can still smell the Ghost Spray, sharp in my nostrils like the citrus our neighbor's dog gets a blast of every time she barks, but with an almost vanilla aftertaste. The can was silver with the words *Most Effective Ghost Spray EVER* spiraling around it in red and black letters.

For less than a year, I fully believed in the power of that can to dispel my demons. It wasn't until Maeve was the same age I had been and wanted the spray too that I looked at it more critically. The silver was matte paint, it turned out, and the writing was clearly done in marker. Underneath, if I squinted hard, I could see the words GLENN 20 DISINFECTANT.

Mum had faked us out. But hey, it worked—because we wanted it to work, I guess. I don't think I slept any worse once I knew the trick.

We'll fix it, promise. XX

That note from Mum was the first handwritten message of my new life. There were many more to come, from Selwyn Floyd or the relatively reticent Prameela Verma.

. . . further neurological and cognitive testing required to determine long-term prognosis . . .

I clung to the idea of plasticity, while Mum took hope from the possibility of remission. No one had come out and said—not in writing, anyway—that spontaneous recovery *wasn't* an option, but the way Prameela looked at me suggested that this wasn't a race she had much of a stake in. She'd already brought up counseling and sign language classes, two concepts I recoiled from, but which Mum enrolled me into regardless.

I felt like a germ on a slide, and that was before the tests even started.

A second stroke was always a rather horrible possibility those first few days. What would go next? I feared losing my vision, leaving me locked in a dark and silent box. Or perhaps the use of my limbs, or my sense of taste and smell. Or my memory. *Which would you rather be?* That was a nightmare from which I awoke only slowly, as test after test came back showing no further changes, for better or for worse, and the drugs did whatever they were doing, and people came and went, writing me still more notes and cards, and sending flowers and inspirational memes that made me want to gag. When I wasn't in the hospital having tests, I was in my room where it all started, feeling irrationally superstitious about my bed and the wardrobe that looms over it, as though sleeping there might risk the curse falling upon me again. When I did sleep, it was on the couch in front of the television, which I set to a YouTube playlist of songs I knew well. That way I could watch the videos and imagine what was happening in the land of audio, from which I had been expelled.

I realize now that I was trying to push through the chaos of recent events and clutch either that last moment of stillness when my personal symphony was still playing, or the first notes of it kicking in again.

Meanwhile, Maeve kept turning the volume down because I had it up too high. To make her point, she shone flashlights in my eyes or waved her hands right in front of my face and then handed me notes saying *This is "loud" for YOU now, right?*

Led from specialist to specialist, I felt again like someone who wasn't really real, a shadow or a ghost of the person I had formerly been. A whole world still existed out there, but I didn't know how to part the veil that separated me from everyone else.

The test I particularly didn't enjoy was the MRI machine. It was like being in a coffin, prematurely interred, and although I couldn't hear the loud noises the machine made, I could certainly feel them. Imagine being inside a steel drum that someone's banging on. My heart tried to beat in time, and I could practically feel the veins in my head become swollen to bursting, shivering on the brink of flooding my brain with darkness, madness, or worse.

When the explosive non-sounds in my skull finished, I felt dizzy to the point of throwing up.

What I wasn't telling anyone, even myself, was that I was terrified. This silence . . . What if my brain didn't reshape itself to hear again? Would I become a ghost permanently chasing a ghost, a memory, a fading echo of the thing that had once filled my life . . . ?

The world was eroding beneath me and around me, and I had nothing solid to cling to but a note from my mother.

• • •

Weirdly, perhaps, it was my other biological parent who made the biggest difference in those early days. Dad wasn't at the hospital, and I don't think it was because Mum wouldn't let him be there. I think he guessed correctly that I needed space more than sympathy, an opportunity to properly process what had happened, and he went in search of something that could help me do that.

It came in the form of the biggest book I had ever seen, wrapped in garish tartan paper with a card that said *Not a scrapbook. Love, Dad.* Despite this reassurance, I unwrapped the parcel with suspicion, unable to imagine what else it could contain but some earnest stand-in for the other vocation he had given me.

I couldn't hear the paper tearing, which still strikes me as tragic. Like losing Christmas, or the smell of toast. Childhood, gone.

Inside was a full orchestral score of Mahler's Tenth Symphony, a work I knew nothing about but was destined to become very familiar with while waiting for my fate to be determined.

The book opened with an introduction that described at some length the ups and downs of the composer's life, leading to the difficult times in which the tempestuous work was written. Gustav Mahler was a fairly complicated Austrian from over a hundred years ago, right when orchestral music was becoming very big, brash, and occasionally brutal (almost metal, you could say). Mahler was greatly influenced by Ludwig van Beethoven, and he wasn't made any less complicated than his hero by falling ill just when he became successful. He died from pneumonia before fully orchestrating this work, which meant it wasn't completed. Like Beethoven, he never heard his last symphony performed.

On the final page of the final movement, he wrote "*für dich leben! für dich sterben!*" and then the pet name of his wife, Alma, who had been cheating on him. So he had that going against him as well.

To live for you! To die for you!

Poor bastard.

Turning to the first page of the score was like opening the door to another world, one written in a language I had never truly experienced before. Not like this. I could read musical notation: Mr. Mackereth had made sure of that. I had never, however, seen notes in such masses, arranged in such complex relationships. They were like letters, and the letters formed words, which formed sentences, which formed paragraphs, all the way up to entire stories. Reading the score was like reading a novel—using symbols to build a version of reality that existed only in my mind.

The first page alone was overwhelming, and most of the instruments were silent. I felt drawn in and repelled at the same time, because what attracted me to this symbolic representation of everything I had lost was the hope that I could experience it again, and this was the very same thing that pushed me away. It *wasn't* the same. Maybe it would *never* be the same.

On the page the music was alive, but at the same time it was dead, like Gustav Mahler's aching heart.

"*Almschi!*" he wrote in agony to his wife under the final notes of the symphony. A cry from a man who had lost everything.

As I scanned the massed staves, his voice sounded loudest among my thoughts and gave me no small comfort.

Someone had been through this kind of pain before me. I wasn't alone.

If it seems strange that a metal-core maniac could be moved by Mahler, well, I have pretty diverse tastes. Still, it seemed strange to me, too. The bigness of the work, which I didn't "hear" so much as "experience" while reading, was something that unfolded in waves as I unpicked melodies, harmonies, and structures that had kept music theorists occupied for a century.

Ultimately, though, I was reaching, straining my mental limbs to snatch the tiniest crumb from the musical table. The futility of trying to resurrect a memory of the last sound I ever heard was possibly matched by that of trying to kickstart my hearing again by will alone—by imagining music solely from a printed score.

I was still telling myself that this, my inability to hear, was a temporary thing. Mahler's score was just a stopgap until *real* music returned. When it did, life would go back to normal: school, social life, girls, music in my ears instead of just my head. I only had to grit my teeth and wait this out, one note-filled page at a time.

Dad understood better than Mum ever did that what I most needed then was not reassurance, but distraction.

Mum's not into music, so I don't think she had a chance of understanding. For her, music is just ambience, and like any other ambience, sometimes it can be too present. One piece of music she does like, though, is a New Age work called "Structures from Silence," by Steve Roach. She plays it when she's stressed—all twenty-eight minutes, thirty-three seconds of it—lying on her back on the living room floor with her eyes tightly closed. She says it's the only thing that settles her mind. I don't know if it works that well, but she certainly played it a lot when she and Dad broke up. My childhood was full of that track's sonic surf crashing on the shores of her unhappiness. The moment it started, Maeve and I would run to our play area, knowing we had half an hour completely to ourselves.

Reading that Mahler score reminded me of Mum's old music. The idea of *structures* from *silence* took on a new kind of profundity. *Maybe,* I thought, *silence doesn't have to be so empty after all.*

Except it is. Perceiving silence differently is the thing. It's all internal. Reading Mahler was exactly like someone handing me a map and me *imagining* the journey as vividly as I could.

Was that a real journey? Define *journey*. Define *real*.

These thoughts kept me at least partially occupied for a full nine days, while I awaited the final diagnosis. When I wasn't trying to remember what my last sounds were, or clutching for any new sounds that might be forthcoming. When I wasn't arguing with my sister, or trying to understand what the specialists were telling me. When I wasn't staring into the gaping empty horror-wardrobe of what life might be like if worse came to worst and my music was turned off forever.

"You can fix this, right?"

We'll fix it, promise. XX

Sometimes a mother's promise is not enough.

VON HATEHOVEN

December 23

What Dad started with Mahler, I continue my own way: engaging with music, sound optional.

My methods have changed over the months. For instance, when I got home from the concert that G bailed on, I plugged my guitar into my laptop and recorded an epic, thirty-minute solo to put me in the mood for sleep. It drew on some of the solos I had memorized *before*—a bit of "Afterlife" here, some "Through the Fire and Flames" there—but on the whole it was improvised, and it sounded pretty good in my head. That was one of the unexpected upsides of being a lead guitarist who can't hear. There was no need for amps or pedals to achieve the ringing awesomeness my timeless licks demanded. Just a guitar in my hands, the unlimited budget of my imagination, and an opportunity to let rip.

Maeve called it aural wankery—and in my darkest hours, I wondered if she was right. What was the point of playing music if no one else experienced it? Mum's hopeless quest to fix everything still went on, in her own way, but she was as out of her depth as I was. And Dad . . . well, there were times I wanted to smash his records and CDs and erase all his files so he'd know what it felt like to be me. Why should he have the chance to hear new music every day when I didn't?

Listen with your eyes, my first counselor told me once.

Fine, I wanted to say, *but how do I scream with my hands?*

The fact that my angst was profoundly selfish didn't lessen its impact. It was lonely there, inside my silent world; all I had to think about was me and my pretend music and my inability to fix anything myself.

After playing each solo, and there were many across those empty weeks, I would put the audio file of the recording in a folder with the others I had saved since losing my hearing. For weeks, I kept them all. It was hard to articulate why, even to myself. Maybe I still hoped that I would hear them one day. Maybe it was just force of momentum.

Since earlier this week when I made G cry, though, I've started deleting them. I tell myself it's a statement. *Hey, see? I don't care whether I hear it or not. It doesn't matter to me.*

Except it does matter. It's totally unfair that my brain will never hear anything ever again, when it still matters to *me.* Couldn't the part that *cares* have been destroyed as well? Life would be so much easier if I didn't care about music or uni or anything else I took for granted before . . . But would I still be me?

That's how I know I'm not really anything like Beethoven: if he wasn't crazy when he died, he must've been when he wrote the Ninth Symphony. How awful to taunt yourself by writing something better than *pretty good*, something truly amazing that everyone but you will hear! That's worse than not finishing something before you die, like Mahler did. To know that a work exists in its complete form, but that you will never experience it . . . What kind of person would willingly do that to themselves?

If not even the composer can partake of the masterwork, there's no point writing a single note.

Is there?

You need to read the postmodernists, G tells me during one of my occasional rants on this subject, two days before Christmas. The audience creates its own experience blah blah.

She's the only person I can talk to about this: how music used to make me feel, how losing music makes me feel, and what steps I could take to get that feeling back. I've learned the hard way not to fake-perform it in front of her, though.

I ask her to explain postmodernism in single-syllable words so I can understand what she's talking about. It takes a while, and I'm still not sure I completely follow the argument.

Something about art being defined by the audience, not the artist. Maybe?

Close enough.

Okay, but where does the audience's "created experience" come from? If two people start with different materials, one sound and one the score, say, how can the different outcomes be considered remotely the same?

I dunno, but if that really matters to you, there must be some way to engineer it in advance. You still remember what sound sounds like, right? Use your imagination.

I already do that. How about people who are born deaf and have never heard a sound at all? What do they experience?

Why are you worried about them all of a sudden?

Because, I sign to myself. This is one of my favorite signs, which maybe says something about how my brain is working at this point. I have *favorite* signs. But what I am really trying to say is: Why should they miss out?

Someone's always going to miss out.

Not if EVERYONE misses out.

That's when it hits me, the real reason why I've been deleting my solos.

Not because I don't care. Because it makes things *even.*

A deleted solo disappears, unheard. No one benefits, no one loses—neither composer nor audience. It's like one of those subatomic particles that pops into existence out of nowhere, explodes into a cascade of smaller bits and bobs that combine and recombine into something very much like the original, and then vanishes back into nothingness. I remember hearing about them in physics and thinking it all sounded very deep.

But it's not. I see that now. It's all actually about revenge.

If I can't hear the world's music, then it in return won't hear mine.

Very noble, G says when I explain this to her. You're my hero, Sadwig von Hatehoven.

But I'm not really paying attention to her banter now. I'm wrapped up in an entirely new thought about music. Absence is a kind of experience. *I'm* certainly feeling something by being denied sound. So maybe the only musical experience a composer could create that can be shared equally by everyone . . . hearing and non-hearing alike . . . is one that's impossible to hear.

Not just recorded and deleted—written and *performed* in such a way that no one could ever experience it the way music is normally experienced. Somehow. The details don't matter right now. I'll work them out. I'll find the hidden shoals that Mr. Mackereth charted. The band will help, and Professor Dorn too—at least, I hope they will. With or without them, I'll bring my discovery up into the light, so no one will ever have to miss out on music—*real* music—ever again.

Screw Beethoven, I tell her in a kind of ecstatic trance. **I'm going to be the next John Cage.**

Good for you.

It bothers me only slightly when she adds, John who?

PART TWO

SAD MUSIC PLAYING

September 13

I don't remember much about the days following my final diagnosis, which was delivered to me during another impersonal, borderline-incomprehensible consultation with all the usual suspects present: Selwyn Floyd's beard, Prameela Verma's impassivity, Mum's anxiety. The words *hearing loss, total,* and *permanent* were like cathedral bells ripped from their moorings, tumbling ponderously but silently in my head. There were no surgical options. No amount of therapy would bring my hearing back. Music was fucking *gone,* and all that remained was me, an empty bell tower fit for pigeons to shit in.

My obsession with the lost notes of my personal symphony came back as intensely as ever. What had I missed, that last night? What poignant fadeout into deathly silence? It killed me that this audience of one would never know.

Maybe if lyrics had been my thing, I would have found a way to fill the void sooner, or at least to express the problem. But sadly, fitting words to music has never worked for me.

Let's talk about passion. What else are you passionate about? Just because music is gone, that doesn't mean nothing's left. Lots of people have more than one passion. Some people even have to choose, say, between being an Olympic athlete or a dancer, because either is a full-time commitment. You lived a rich and full life when you could hear, Simon. Your life can still be rich and full. It IS rich and full, even if you don't see that right now.

This important message was delivered by my first counselor, Sandra Mack, a stunningly beautiful woman with yellow streaks through white hair—or perhaps the other way around—a nose ring, and the upper tendrils of a vine tattoo showing above the front of her overalls. Her opening gambit was to ask me about my tatts. *Are we bonding now?* I wanted to type back, disliking her immediately.

She continued, relentlessly:

My dad is an artist, a painter. That's not all he's into, though. In fact, he says it's not the work of other painters that inspires him. It's books. I think art is like that, even if we're not aware of it. Being inspired by what we produce is a bit like, well, cannibalism, or incest, if you don't mind me being a bit gross. And there's that awful line about infidelity: doesn't matter where you get your appetite, as long as you eat at home. Whatever gets the juices flowing, right?

So what else are you passionate about, Simon? That's

your path through this. Because "this" is not the end. It's a new beginning. You'll see that one day, trust me.

What do you say in reply to this?

Sandra and I communicated via our laptops in an office at Deaf Solutions, a community organization for people with hearing problems of all kinds, including those like me whose worlds are newly silent. Its headquarters are in a small office building refurbished with flashing-light doorbells, telephones, and other visual aids. I was introduced to Sandra as part of the next stage of my treatment, which was to get used to the fact that I would never hear again, something I was reluctant to deal with in the usual ways. Mum insisted I go, at Prameela's suggestion, in order to find a way forward.

We need our own way to talk, you and I, Sandra said in our first session. What would make you most comfortable?

We settled on the laptops but not using email. Instead we accessed a shared document in the cloud that we both typed into. That way, I could follow her cursor on my screen and watch the platitudes flow magically from it without having to look at her at all.

Dammit, she was beautiful. I couldn't help wondering where the rest of that tattoo went, which distracted me from my misery, so that was something.

Well, I used to be passionate about books too, I guess, when I was a kid. Since then I mainly watch movies and TV.

Great! That's something.

But subtitles suck. And I really hate it when they say things like "sad music playing." Why even bother? It's futile. Like painting by numbers but without the paint, just the numbers.

I understand.

How can you? You're not deaf.

My parents are, and so's my boyfriend. That's why I became an interpreter and then a counselor. I know how hard it can be for the Deaf in a world built by and for hearing people . . . but that doesn't mean only hearing people can live in it.

What if I don't want to?

If you're feeling depressed—

No, not that. Everywhere I look I'm reminded of what's missing. People talking to each other with their voices, wearing headphones, answering doorbells, waking up to alarms . . . What if the world hurts too much? What if it's easier to hide from it?

There's a thriving Deaf community all around you. You probably pass Deaf people every day, sit next to them on the bus, cross the road with them—

I just wish there was somewhere I could go to get away from it all. Be alone. Work this out by myself.

I don't think that would really help. You're a smart guy, Simon. I feel like I can say this to you: your problem is a sense of disconnection from your life, because you can no longer hear. Being *more* disconnected will only make things worse. You tell me you feel like everything you ever knew is irrelevant—or even worse, made painful because of the way things are now. There are reminders of music and sound all around you. But I want you to know that the way things are now doesn't change everything. You're still you, and your world is still there. It's just different. In some ways, you'll find it to be more exciting. Trust me.

She kept saying that. *Trust me.* I didn't listen. I couldn't. Listening meant words and sounds, and they were lost to me. Reading text on a screen felt about as real as reading a score instead of listening to the symphony—which was distracting for a while but ultimately unsatisfying. I was sick of the facsimile. I wanted the real thing, and she couldn't give it to me.

BLACKMOD

December 26

Sandra was right, though, on more levels than I was prepared to admit, then. To her, or to myself.

I'd been seeing a girl called Shari on and off when I had my stroke. It was she who habituated me to using texts to communicate with hearing friends, although Shari would hate that this was her legacy, because, well, you know. Ultimately her text-talking trick was a quick fix that did nothing to address the actual problem. I wasn't ready to give up the sounds of things just because there existed ways to get by without them. The smell of popcorn isn't the same minus the sound of it popping. The feel of guitar strings under my fingertips is no substitute for the riff from "Black Dog."

Then there's sex.

If you'd asked me beforehand, I'd have said it'd be easy—it's all physical, right? Who needs words? But the whole thing is overwhelming without the other participant's voice to bind it together. At least it was for me.

This was something Shari never understood. Or maybe

she just wasn't the right person for me. The night she tried to shag me on the couch, while music videos screened in the background, was a disaster. I couldn't deal with it—didn't know how loud we were being, who might overhear, how to ask her what she wanted, if she was even enjoying it . . .

Turns out when gripped with uncertainty, you need words more than ever. Touch, taste, smell, and sight are all great, but I hadn't learned yet how to properly manage them alone. Shari was a freight train bearing down on me in a dark tunnel, and I didn't know which way to dodge. Talk about performance anxiety.

There was no way we could text about this, certainly not during. We kept trying to make it work, though, thanks to hormones and habit. And maybe out of a sense of obligation. I certainly thought it was helping her, and she probably thought it was helping me. Turns out it wasn't helping either of us, in the long run.

If intimacy is a problem, having a group chat with my two closest friends via social media feels just as authentic as ever. We're all equal under the eyes of Twitter.

After the obligatory Grandma-got-me-socks-for-Christmas conversation, I decide to present my big idea to them: music that no one can hear.

You want to what now?

You heard the man. Play music for the deaf.

That's not really what I meant.

Don't they already have music? If you turn it up loud enough?

Yes, but that's just doof doof doof, Alan. It's like throwing out the food and licking an empty plate.

What kind of food? Vegetarian could be an improvement.

Come on, hear me out. The deaf AND hearing get the same experience. No one misses anything. Everyone goes home happy.

Can't do it.

Gotta try.

It'll be paintings for the blind next.

Called sculpture, dude. Let the Drip finish before you cut him down. It's only fair.

I've known Roo and Sad Alan since primary school. They call me the Drip because of my surname, Rain. That's what we tell people, anyway. Roo, supposedly short for Rooster, does have an amazing red quiff, and Alan the longest face I've ever seen, but the secret meanings of our nicknames are very different. And obscene.

We went our separate ways for a bit, thanks to parents sending us to different high schools, but a love of music brought us back together once we started playing in earnest. Me, guitar and the occasional growl. Roo, bass and vocals. Sad Alan, drums.

Together, Blackmod—the latest of many band names.

It wasn't our intention to start a band at all, really. We just wanted to make loud noises together and get out of playing sports. We didn't even perform original songs for a long time, unless you can call unstructured, aggressively incoherent improvisations "originals," which I guess they did in the 1960s, when Dad was a kid. We practiced in our garage. Mum made us wear ear protection, because, although the space was lightly insulated to spare the rest of the world, the walls and ceiling were bare and the floor was concrete, so our sonic attacks returned on us largely unimpeded. These sessions left me feeling breathless, as though the sheer volume of our brilliance had shaken the oxygen right out of the air.

I liked being in the garage, where no one could see us being our true selves. It was inevitable, though, that one of us would want to perform live, and that one was Sad Alan. He had a crush on a girl called Courtney, who liked live music. His plan was to get a gig, any gig, to increase his chances with her, and Roo was onboard with this plan. I was the one who had to be convinced. We would need a venue, for a start. Then a set list, not to mention at least one original song, preferably not comprised entirely of licks nicked from our favorite bands. A look. And hey, a name. Surely we'd need that!

Every objection I raised was met efficiently, with determination and good cheer. They weren't going to let me rain on Sad Alan's parade before Courtney had a chance to.

Thus was born Scrote Punch. Not one of the immortal names of show business, but impactful. Pardon the pun.

Our first proper song, "Malevolent Machinery," was equally impactful, if only for being terrible. I think it's okay to be terrible, though, when you're starting out. It means you're taking chances. You only have to worry if you *stay* terrible.

That's what Dad told me once, and he would know. *Working out when to give up,* he says, *that's the hard thing.*

GEORGE-WHO-LOVES-COFFEE

September 23

Three weeks after my stroke, I attended my first deaf class, but with a sense of obligation instead of the *this is a new beginning, yay!* that Sandra would rather her clients embraced.

Because none of us had planned to be there—who would? —we each had a different way of reacting. The guy with the thick handlebar mustache, a forklift operator whose years working in a factory had finally done in his hearing, watched everything closely and reproduced the signs with mechanical precision belying the look of his leathery, knuckled hands. The woman with bouffant, dyed fake-natural hair came bearing voluminous notes and a repertoire of apologetic expressions ready for when she got things wrong; she had lost her hearing from a bad case of the flu, of all things. The guy in his twenties who hit on me once seemed almost excited to learn this new skill, engaging with an exuberance that was desperate at times. Or maybe that was just me projecting. He was a recreational diver who timed an ascent wrong and blew his ears out.

Deaf class was where I met G. As I say, we didn't hit it off at first. I was shy, she surly. When I hid in the corner, she resorted to gestures, often rude ones. These, we quickly learned, didn't count.

Our teacher was a cheerful deaf woman in her fifties who, via a mixture of handouts, projections, and whiteboard scribbles, did her best to bring us up to speed. Her name was Hannah, and I would've liked her more had our circumstances been different. At the very least, she gave me a rocking deaf name. The first thing she taught us was the difference between gestures and signing.

Gesture is any form of nonverbal communication, like shrugging, giving someone the middle finger, or blowing a kiss. Those early days, my home life was conducted almost entirely through gestures, every exchange an elaborate, torturous variation on "pass the salt." Deaf and hearing alike use gestures. They're not the same as *signing*, though, which is a full-on language, with rules.

G was a master at expressing her disdain for Hannah and her rules by means of posture (slouching, mainly), proxemics (where she stood in relation to others, usually apart), hand position (biting her fingernails so neither her fingers nor her expression was clear), and so on.

At first it was intimidating, particularly if she and I were paired together. Later, I found it amusing. Perhaps because it was clear I wasn't enjoying classes either, she seemed to settle on me as the least irritating person available.

People are building sign-language gloves, you know, she texted me once from the other side of the room during a ten-minute break in class. Like dictation software but for deaf people. The machine turns the signs into words on a screen so ordinary people can read them.

How does that help us? We can't sign.

Ah, you see, that's the best bit. We don't need to. We can still talk, right? Ordinary dictation software can transcribe it, so deaf people can read what we're saying. Then the gloves transcribe what they're saying back to us. No need for us to learn sign language at all!

Could work. It'd all have to be done through computers, though. Or phones.

That's where augmented reality comes in.

Now I know you're messing with me.

Someone has to. I mean, have you looked in the mirror lately?

That stung a little, because I wasn't sure how she meant it. Was she saying I was sloppy-looking? My hair was long and straight and not easy to keep in condition. I had a goat patch on my chin, but nothing as protuberant as Tutankhamun or the bassist from System of a Down. The rest I kept clean-shaven.

Or was she talking about my clothes? I'm a jeans-and-band-T-shirt kind of guy, with Converses or something chunkier if I'm in a particularly metal mood. The money I don't spend on my guitar goes on my feet, mainly. All those shifts at KFC were totally worth it.

So to be dissed, potentially, by this hot stranger, possibly the last one who'd ever try to talk to me in my isolated new world . . . well, I wanted to know exactly what for.

I asked her, in response to her mirror crack, **Have you ever listened to a recording of yourself talking?**

Not lately. Duh.

Of course not. Before.

Who hasn't?

It's weird because we're used to hearing the sound of our voices conducted from our voiceboxes to our ears via the bones of our skull and jaw. That's why we sound so bassy and warm. We all have this overinflated sense of how good we sound, because we never hear ourselves right.

Is that true? Huh. Interesting. But who says the way other people hear us is the "right" way to hear us?

My point exactly. Mirrors are the voice recorders of the eyes.

Wait. Wouldn't they be the echoes of the eyes? Or wouldn't seeing yourself in a video be the same as a voice recording?

Are you always this pedantic?

Only when someone says something wrong, but still interesting.

I'll take that as a compliment.

That was the first time she smiled at me, and I felt something flutter through me. It didn't feel like passion, then, but it certainly felt real.

OMGS AND WTFS

October 2

Loving music and being a musician are two very different things, as different as loving to watch a sport and playing it. Which is not to say that being an observer of art is in any way passive or meaningless: G was totally right on that score, when she told me to read the postmodernists. Anyone possessing the right senses can immediately engage with art—training, practice, or commitment not required.

But I guess it depends on how you define *musician*. If I remain committed to my earlier proposition, that *there's no such thing as unmusical sound,* then maybe there's no such thing as an unmusical musician, either. You can pick up a violin and make the most godawful noise, and it *counts*. It must, or my thesis unravels.

A musician, Dad tells me when I ask him, is someone who engages with the music industry. Be it in a band or behind a mixing desk or as an agent . . . However they're doing it, they're adding to the great pooled experience that is *music*.

Because music, he says, is about the audience. If people aren't experiencing it too, it's "solipsistic twaddle."

"Aural wankery," in Maeve's words.

Dad has some experience in the field. His name, Bengt Bengtsson, is slightly recognizable, him having been in a band that had a brief window of fame in the late 1980s. Contact was a blatant Depeche Mode knockoff whose first album, *Day of the Dolls,* features their sole hit song: "Tokyo Go." Its jarringly peppy chorus occasionally pops up in the background of movies set around that time. Part of the ambience, with a slight hint of mockery for times when people didn't know any better. It has a pretty good synth bass line, which was all Dad. His hair was bright blue back then, and very, very high.

Mum insists they didn't hook up because he was tall, handsome, and in a band. I think they might have, because she's so insistent about denying it. Also, later, when he had no hair and a string of albums no one listened to, they broke up.

More likely, though, they broke up because Mum doesn't really care about music. Oh, and Dad is a hopeless husband.

Let me make it clear that during my first sign language lessons I wasn't pursuing *George-who-loves-coffee,* and not only because I was still seeing Shari. Technically. Perhaps we could have worked through our sex problems, but communication wasn't our thing even when I could hear. It would be fair to say, in fact, that we never really talked at all. Not properly. We were a walking cliché. I had my friends, and when she talked to me, mainly to complain about me spending too much time on the band, I tuned it out because it wasn't anything I cared to hear. Her chatter and my silence performed the same function, to distract us from the fact that we had nothing in common.

When I lost my hearing that September, her voice was another part of the symphony that I hadn't noticed until it was gone. What remained between us gained a kind of poignancy as a result, and I think she felt some of that too. She was *there,* which was worth something, and she wrote me many, many text messages, mostly about what was happening at school interspersed with OMGs and WTFs and SURELY SOMEONE CAN DO SOMETHINGs, but occasionally just to see how I was doing and if she could help. She isn't a monster. She was in her own version of a hard place.

Turns out boys with sad eyes who just sit in their room playing guitar with the amp turned off are no fun. Who knew?

When Maeve, whose friend she had been in primary school, passed on the news that Shari had been seen kissing a footballer called Jude Lee at a final-exam party on the one-month anniversary of my stroke, I was not terribly surprised. I'd sensed the crisis coming.

Which is not to say that I wasn't hurt. I felt miserable about it, actually. Not Gustav Mahler territory, but still.

"Way to kick a guy when he's down," I told Maeve, the bearer of bad tidings.

It's your own fault, she said via a small whiteboard she had taken to carrying around in case I needed to be annoyed.

"How do you figure that?"

Well, maybe if you weren't being such a miserable, useless shit, Shari wouldn't be off pashing other boys.

"Thanks. You've made me feel so much better."

Is that my job? I must not have received the memo.

"You're my sister!"

Exactly. Not your mother, counselor, or girlfriend. Someone's got to get you off your arse and on with your life. Such as it's worth.

I wrote *Fuck you!* on the whiteboard and stomped off to my room, where I blasted out another blistering solo into the void of my hard drive. But she had a point. Lots of people lose their hearing. It's inevitable that some of them are musicians. Evelyn Glennie is probably the best example, so famous even Mum has heard of her, thanks to the Adelaide Festival. She started losing her hearing at the age of eight and was totally deaf by twelve. That hasn't stopped her from performing on the world stage as a percussionist and a composer.

Reading about her on Wikipedia later that night gave me the impetus to get off the couch. If Evelyn Glennie could give deafness the finger, why couldn't I? Sandra would've been proud!

Also, success is the best form of revenge, they say. Suppose I did keep playing and Blackmod took off . . . ? Well, Shari would rue the day she ever cheated on Simon Rain.

SCROTE PUNCH

3 Years Earlier

The hardest thing for me about sign language is this: it's only partly about signing.

Not so long ago, people used to think the Deaf were mentally deficient. Partly this was because hearing people only interpreted the *signs,* which was like translating Russian to English but glossing over every word that contained a *K,* resulting in speech that looked disjointed, simplistic, and, well, dumb.

There's more to Auslan than the signs, and that's . . . a challenge, particularly for a shy person like me. Nuance and entire meanings are conveyed via body language and facial expression: ignoring those parts is like deadening a speaking person's tongue with anesthetic. Embracing them, though, means opening up in ways that feel unnatural. Dangerous, even. Every grimace, eyebrow raise, or head tilt is a window into your soul.

When you're saying "sad," for instance, you don't just make the sign for *sad* with your hands. You put on the face and act out the emotion. You *are* the emotion—for the purposes of communication, yes, but you can't help feeling it a little as well.

I do, anyway. *Hungry, afraid, sleepy, strong* . . . When was the last time you had a conversation that didn't touch at least tangentially on something emotional or triggering? How you *hate* the way G doesn't respond to your texts sometimes. Or Roo's sneakers smell like *arse*. Or you'd *kill* to hear the new TesseracT single. Or whatever *fucking* thing . . .

Everyone has details they just don't want to reveal.

And, well . . . I say I'm shy, which most people don't believe. It's not that I don't like people. I just like them in small doses, and I like to control what they see of me.

And that's why sign language is so confronting to me. I'm not acting a part. I'm acting *me*.

It's also why my first live performance was so terrifying. There was Simon Rain, a kid who had been playing in private with his best mates, suddenly thrust into a literal spotlight and expected to shred in front of a sea of strangers. There was nothing to like about that scenario. I pictured a thousand ways the night would end me. Memory blackout. Electrocution. Bladder failure. Catastrophic trouser collapse. Each as unlikely as the other.

I am at my most inventive when I scare myself shitless.

Roo and Sad Alan pushed me ahead of them onto the stage. The light was dazzling, and it was much warmer than I had expected. I was glad I'd worn my ripped jeans and a Death Meal T-shirt (our "look" being teen wannabe hardcore), because otherwise I would've been sweat-logged in an instant. As it was, my eyes felt foggy, and I stumbled, momentarily losing my way.

Muscle memory from sound check guided me to my guitar, and its familiar weight gave me an anchor. I turned to confront a sea of faces—one of them *did* belong to the crushable Courtney, it turned out, and the knowledge that this would make Sad Alan the nervous one pulled me right out of my anxiety. I was doing this for him, right? I couldn't fuck up.

Click, hum. The guitar was live. I raised my pick and power-chorded the opening notes of our second original song, "Thy Ken." A staccato blast of noise, more percussive than melodic.

The crowd responded with a mixture of cheers and jeers (there are always "friends" who think booing is funny, except when they're on the receiving end). The response wasn't unanimous, but that didn't matter. They had *responded.*

Sad Alan, the color of his skin camouflaged perfectly against the black-sheet backdrop, *boom-tish*ed to signal he was ready. Roo rumbled on the E-string.

I played the opening riff again, and off we went, just like we'd rehearsed in the garage so many times, but this time with the sound blasting away from us into a kinetic human void, and the smell of sweat other than our own thick in our nostrils, and all manner of unpredicted upsets, such as feedback and noisy cabling and our foldback dropping out at one point, and the echo from the far end of the Jade Monkey trying to drag me off beat in the slow sections . . .

Scrote Punch was onstage. It didn't matter if anyone else liked us, because we were having a good time, sharing something we enjoyed with a world that seemed to care, at least partially, because someone had turned up. And they weren't leaving. Not all of them, anyway.

We played for half an hour, then we came off. Opening act of five. *The only way is up,* I remember thinking as I left the stage, sizzling with adrenaline. The shy boy had had his first taste of performing. He had finally met a real, live audience, and it was love at first sight.

"THY KEN"

October 3

Someone once said, *Show me a person capable of nobility in the face of rejection and I'll show you someone who secretly wanted out anyway.* Me, I didn't want out—not from my relationship with Shari, problematic though it was, and not from the hearing world, either. Her breaking up with me doubled down a sense of complete social expulsion, the feeling that I was being squeezed forcibly out of the world.

My oldest friends visited as well as tweeted, of course. Roo and Sad Alan sat on the couch and passed me corn chips and commiserated via text. They joked about making up our own sign language that no one else could understand. We watched silent movies on YouTube while I missed the tinkly piano music and stewed in my misfortune.

The day after being dumped, I was the first to raise the one thing the three of us hadn't discussed yet.

So . . . Blackmod.

Don't feel bad about us, Drip. We're cool.

Uh, what?

You know, it was fun while it lasted, and we don't blame you. It's just one of those things.

Let the man finish, Alan. I don't think he's apologizing.

I was going to suggest a rehearsal. Maybe write a new song. Did you really think I was going to break up the band?

Well . . . yeah.

Blackmod means everything to me. We've got to play!

But—

Shut up, Alan. Having a one-armed drummer didn't stop Def Leppard, did it?

Hey, "Deaf Leopard"—

We're not changing the band name again. Let's just do this!

Sad Alan's assumption was forgivable, but I felt wounded all the same. Why did me not being able to hear mean the band was over and done with?

Furiously, I led them straight into the garage and went through the usual motions of plugging into the amp and turning up the gain.

No click. No hum.

The absence of both hit particularly hard, and suddenly I found myself full of an emotion I wasn't ready to define. It made me breathe hard. My pulse raced.

"Thy Ken," I said, knowing they could hear even if I couldn't, and launched into the opening riff, as I had that first time on stage three years earlier. They joined in, blowing away a mournful thickness in my throat. I was immediately struck by the deep frequencies of drum and bass as though a fresh wind had blown through the room. The band felt just as vibrant and vital as ever.

Musical instruments are definitely alive. The guitar my father gave me seemed to shiver in my arms the moment I first strummed it. My black Schecter Omen now shook with sympathetic vibrations from the other instruments in the room. At that moment, I truly understood what Dad was on about. Music is at heart a collaboration between composer, performer, and audience. Those roles aren't always separate—in this case, I was partly all three—but however it's arranged, it's an ecosystem, not a matter of mechanically following a set of instructions in order to create a series of pressure waves in the air that achieves a desired result. It's unpredictable, unexpected, unfathomable.

Music is not a thing you're doing. It's a process, a thing you're being.

That day in the garage, I was being it in a different way than ever before, and it was . . . Well, it wasn't as brilliant as it had been. But it made me aware of how bored I had been without it. The counseling sessions and deaf classes were exhausting, as was trying to cope with life's new challenges, but they weren't *stimulating*. Playing with my friends was *stimulating*.

"Thy Ken" roared to a brutal finish. The three of us fell back, grinning. I felt exhausted, like I'd had the best sex of my life. Don't judge me. My elation in that moment was genuine.

Just because I had lost my girlfriend along with a small oyster of brain tissue didn't mean that I had lost absolutely everything.

Sad Alan reached for his phone and typed something. Mine buzzed in my pocket.

I've never heard you play like that.

Some of my elation ebbed. Did he mean out of tune or off beat? I had felt nothing but perfection. "How?"

Angry.

It's cool, said Roo. *You've got every right.*

I sure do, I remember thinking, and, *Yeah, they'd better be cool with it*. They were my best friends. They had to take me as I came.

But now my elation was gone. In its place was the feeling I had had before, when plugging in my guitar. Now Alan had named it, I knew it for what it was, and it didn't feel good.

FOUR MINUTES AND CHANGE

December 26

The sense that my friends are unable to understand what I'm going through, even though they understand *me* perfectly well, is very present when I continue trying to explain my big idea.

Mimes? You want us to stand on stage together and be mimes!?

No. Pretending to play isn't the point. It's playing SILENCE.

Jesus. Do we even need to be there?

Yes, or it's just an empty stage.

And the difference is . . . ?

The difference is that the room isn't empty. There's an audience. There's a band. There's music, only it's silent. Get it?

I get that whatever happened to your head was worse than we thought.

It's like that piece of music where the audience makes the noise. Is that right, Drip? No one actually plays anything, but there's still background sound. That sound is the music.

Kind of . . . but not really.

The world has come a long way since the premiere of John Cage's *4'33"*, in which a pianist sits at a piano and does nothing for three movements while the audience listens to whatever ambient noise happens to fill the auditorium. The piece is often brought up as a joke, but really it's utterly brilliant. *4'33"* is not like Beethoven's Ninth, in which all the notes are laid out and an orchestra just has to play them in the right order. In Cage's masterwork, there are no notes, and the audience—the *world*—is the orchestra. Every time it's performed, it's different.

The true genius of the piece is in the title: *4'33"*. There's no traditional musical performance, but it's perfectly structured by having a time limit. It's not random in that regard. It's not *Four Minutes and Change*. John Cage sat down and *wrote* the damn thing exactly the way he wanted. He put years of thought into it. He *composed* it.

So how can it not be music?

Because neither the musician nor the instrument is making a sound, you might say. Isn't that what needs to happen for there to be anything we can call music?

People have been debating this question for decades now. It's not the debate I want to have with my oldest friends.

The background noise will just be something hearing

people can hear, and if they're distracted by it, well, that's a shame, but it won't be part of the music.

So what is?

The music would be . . . the music. I'm still working on that part. And really, it's not the most important thing, not today. I just want to know that you'd be part of this. That you'd be there, if it ever happens. Even if you think it's wrong.

Or fucking mental.

At the same time as I'm attempting to enlist the support of Blackmod, I'm sounding out someone who knows much more about this kind of experiment than I ever will. Professor Dorn isn't terribly approachable under the best of circumstances, though. Emails, I've learned, prompt autoreplies warning of delays due to the constraints of academia, the demands of various projects, and frequent physiotherapy for workplace injuries. And maybe she'll tell me I'm fucking mental too. But she at least knows from my attempts to get into her course how determined I am.

So, Rain, you want to write music for the deaf now, she replies to my email, three days after I had sent it. *I guess that's an improvement on your last submission. Tell me why.*

This is hard because I know from bitter experience that she will call me on any halfhearted bullshit. Being vague won't work, and neither will hiding behind jargon. I have to be blunt and sincere and, above all, interesting. She's like G, which makes me wonder if deep down I dig the challenge.

You're the one who got me into John Cage. I don't think he went far enough.

This time there's no delay between my communication and her reply.

The man who said, "Everything we do is music"—you don't think he went far enough?

He also said, "Every something is an echo of nothing." What if nothing is the whole point, and the something only gets in the way?

So you did read the book I recommended. Well done, I suppose. You're saying, what does it matter if music is composed of sounds or not? Maybe the sounds interfere with what music really is, underneath. Yes?

Yes, Professor D.

So tell me what music really is.

I prepared this answer in advance.

Music is in three parts: the idea, the execution, and the audience. Who says what form the execution has to take?

No one. Especially not someone who can hear to someone who can't. That would be discrimination, Rain, although I'm pretty sure the university's antidiscrimination policy manual is under one of the legs of my desk . . .

If* 4'33" *creates a space in which the world supplies the performance, why not a piece where the space IS the performance?

This time there is a pause. I wait anxiously at my computer, biting my thumbnails. If I get up and walk away, I won't see her reply, which comes twenty minutes later.

Do you think you can actually make something of this?

Yes. I want to.

Well, hurrah for you.

I need to.

You still need a portfolio, you mean, if you hope to study in my composition class. And I, as it happens, need works for the undergraduate concert in June. Perhaps you'll get to stage your little experiment there, if you can supply me with something in time. No promises. Submissions are due next month.

Suddenly, this is seeming much realer than I expected. Originally, I intended to write a piece for Blackmod to perform in a bar, not at university . . .

Does this mean you'll help?

As much as I can. I'll need to see a proposal, which necessitates talking about what this actually is. I don't think you really know yet. Arrange for an interpreter, and let's meet.

I can't agree to that, but I don't want to explain why. That would mean confessing that my knowledge of sign language is depressingly deficient. Skipping deaf class has held me back in a way that, for the first time, makes me feel slightly ashamed.

Maybe we can stick to email for now?

All right, but it's touch-and-go how long my hands will hold out. I can't do this all day, you know.

Professor Dorn's repetitive strain injury is a source of constant complaint. I see barriers to communication everywhere now. It's amazing people talk at all.

THE MARS SCENARIO

October 7

I regard this as progress, Simon. Super to see you practicing again, even if it did provoke feelings that weren't universally positive. Few experiences are universally anything, I'm sure you'd agree. You still have questions. The answers won't all come to you at once, but they're waiting for you. Be open to them, and they will come.

God, I hated when Sandra talked like this. I resisted the urge to introduce her to Sad Alan; a few days ago, at the first practice of the poststroke Blackmod, I had shown him the selfie I'd taken with her, and he had declared himself instantly in love.

To say that I was not in love with Sandra would be the definition of an understatement.

Oh, come on.

You sound so skeptical. I bet you're thinking: how much longer do I have to wait for these answers? What do I do until they come?

Uh, no.

What, then?

It's too hard to explain.

I was feeling the same anger I had felt while playing "Thy Ken," something I definitely didn't want to share, because I knew she'd try to talk me out of it. Anger was all I had, after Shari.

Okay, Simon, let's change the subject. What about Mars? I read recently that the air pressure there is so low that sound hardly carries at all. So if people ever live on Mars, they might as well be deaf.

Unless they're wearing spacesuits, I said, playing along with wary relief. At least she'd stopped digging into my feelings with a dental pick.

Right, or never leave their habitats, those little inflatable houses where they do all their experiments. If they stay in there, they'll be fine.

Until they go back home to Earth, where they belong.

Exactly. But what if they can't go back home? Wouldn't it be better if they could learn how to live without spacesuits?

Oh, god. I'm the Martian in this scenario.

And you have a choice: you can pretend that everything is exactly the way it used to be, only your suit has a leak in it. You can patch it. You can go back into your habitat. But there'll always be another leak, no matter how you try to preserve the plastic protecting you. Your bubble is going to deflate eventually. Why not accept that and adapt to the new world right now? Learn to breathe that air and go exploring. You never know what wonders you might find!

If I actually was on Mars, I would agree with you. But I'm not. None of that is real, and I'm not giving up the band.

I'm not talking about the band, Simon.

Or music.

I'm not talking about music either.

Then what!? Help me out here!

That's when she did something she hadn't done in any of our sessions before. She rested her hands on the laptop and spoke to me with her mouth. The way her lips moved would've made Sad Alan swoon, but I could only guess what she was saying.

"I'm not dead," I said aloud through grinding teeth.

The look she gave me said as clearly as words, *You know that's not what I said.*

"And you doing that isn't helping," I told her.

She made the sign for *What?*

I imitated her *you-know* expression. "Everything." *Being so smug,* mostly.

She signed something I didn't understand. I just stared furiously at her until she typed on the computer:

Tell me, Simon, please.

"All I can tell you is that this is getting me nowhere," I said, scooping up my laptop and throwing it into my backpack. Sandra waved her hands to get my attention, but I ignored her and left the room, filled with a rage I could never have expressed.

In the reception area, Mum glanced up in surprise and put her magazine aside: my session wasn't due to finish for another ten minutes.

Are you okay? she signed.

I exited the building, not meeting her eye. Her stare was too . . . parental. Too worried, too judgmental, too full of questions.

"Take me to Dad's," I said, slumping into the passenger seat. Mum's car is an ancient red Civic that smells of stale pastries and socks. Maeve and I share the Civic she owned before this one, which is so dire it defies description. It's more rust than car now, I think.

Mum pulled pen and paper from her handbag, and I moved quickly to cut her off.

"I don't want to talk about it."

She settled for patting my shoulder, and I shrugged her hand away, hoping she couldn't see the acid tears filling my eyes. The car came to life underneath me, and then we were moving, jerking into traffic. Everything was pointless. I was choking in a cloud so thick and heavy it might collapse on me at any moment. I had to lash out at someone.

I fumbled for my phone and texted Maeve. We hadn't spoken since our argument about me being a miserable useless shit.

You're such a bitch. How can you side with Shari? She's the one who dumped a deaf guy.

Maeve must have been waiting by the phone.

Is that what you are now?

I wrapped both hands around my phone and ground it so hard into my forehead it left a dent. That was the closest I would let myself come to screaming.

PRIVATE RADIO

December 29

Being mental has never stopped us before, Drip. A gig's a gig. And we get paid, right?

Maybe?

You want musicians to mime your music or whatever it is, you gotta pay them.

All right, all right. You'll get paid.

Great. Easiest six-pack I'll ever earn.

I feel a bit of seasonal cheer when Roo and then Sad Alan finally sign up for a performance that might never happen of music that no one will ever hear. Where that cheeriness comes from, exactly, I don't immediately know. It's not like I'm going to be blasting those chords from "Thy Ken" into a crowd. It's not like I'm going to feel the organic and very powerful connection between me and my guitar, my guitar and the amp, and my amp and the speakers, as though I'm woven into a strange cybernetic organism that's somehow using me rather than the other way around . . .

Or maybe it's exactly that, I think over the following days, *only it's a different kind of connection and a different audience to connect with.* Music is the thing, the thing that binds me to my instrument and my instrument to the crowd. If we just change the instrument to something that doesn't require noise, while at the same time maintaining that connection . . .

You're self-sabotaging again.

G emerges via text after five days of silence to respond to a long message I sent her last night, outlining my latest confused thoughts and asking her what she's doing on New Year's Eve. It may seem weird that I talk to her electronically even when she doesn't respond, but I know she'll tell me to fuck off if ever she gets tired of it. I assume she's out there somewhere, tuning in to our private radio station, even if I'm the only one transmitting most of the time.

Unless you're actively trying to scare me off . . .

I take this as the invitation it is.

Well, golly gee, G. I thought I already had.

Ho ho ho. Life has been complicated.

Yeah, I get that. Tell me what you're doing right now.

I'm wondering what's in this for you.

How much detail would you like me to go into?

No. This impossible music thing of yours.

The new John Cage, remember?

I remember. But what REALLY?

This silences me for a moment. *What really?* With Scrote Punch, the answer had been easy to define. I did it for Sad Alan and Courtney—who did get together in the end, but only long enough for my idiot friend to realize that he preferred the fantasy to the reality. From then on, it was for me, tentatively probing the previously unexpressed desire to step into an arena that sporty blokes normally occupy: showing off and competing and, yes, being noticed by girls, because it turned out that with time and a lot of practice, we stopped being *completely* terrible. All the other bands were an extension of that theme.

What if I don't want to tell you? I text back.

If you can't tell me, who are you going to tell?

There's my counselor.

Are you back seeing KO again? I thought you said he was stupid.

He isn't, really. Better than Sandra, anyway. He just makes me feel stupid.

Not wanting to talk doesn't make you stupid.

I thought guys weren't supposed to be able to.

Men have plenty of problems, but that's not one of them. Have you been on Reddit lately?

That isn't talking.

So show me what is. Give me the particulars. Give me WHAT REALLY. Think of it as a late Xmas present.

I have to do something when you're not around, don't I?

You mean you don't sit holding your phone all day and all night, creating playlists I'll never hear?

Uh, maybe that last part.

Try again, bro. Third time's the charm.

It's so difficult to tap out. My thumbs feel suddenly gigantic, like they'll mash down on the wrong letters if I don't try very hard.

Music, performing music, gives my life meaning.

There you go. Shockingly articulate as well as completely obvious.

Sorry to disappoint you. You wanted it.

I did. I do. And please, no jokes about that, or you will disappoint me.

Heaven forfend! *crosses out brilliant quip about voids needing to be filled*

groan Why do I even bother?

Why do you, exactly? WHY REALLY etc.

You want to hear what I've not been telling you?

Sure.

The thought of seeing you again makes me afraid.

Of what?

Of what might happen.

Particulars, please.

She goes silent for a while. I wait, not wanting to risk breaking this fragile link she's reestablished. She'll come back in her own time, sooner rather than later, I hope, and she does.

Of everything. And if you think I'm talking about sex, I'm not talking about sex. Perhaps I should make that clear. I'm not afraid of sex. In fact, I think we should have sex. You and me. That would be a good thing. If you would like to. What do you think about that?

I read the message four times to make absolutely sure I'm

understanding her correctly. Behind the words there's a definite impression that she has been sitting wherever she is tapping out the letters as carefully as I am, maybe deleting the whole thing a couple of times before hitting *send*. My reply needs to be delicate and nuanced in return. Adult.

Hell yes.

Well, I'm glad that's established. Would you like to come over?

Um . . . now?

Yes. But no phones. Promise me.

I promise.

While I text with one hand, I'm looking for a clean T-shirt with the other and trying to remember if I had a shower this morning.

You do realize I have no idea where you live?

That's okay. I'm not there right now.

She gives me an address. It's in the city, in a corner of the Square Mile far from any clubs, restaurants, or apartments. I click the link for a map . . . frown . . . and drop back onto the bed as understanding sinks in.

She's in a hospital.

PART THREE

SILENT SIGNS

December 29

English has silent letters. They're inaudible, but if you take them out of a word, the whole meaning is changed. *This is not a knot,* for instance. *The lamb is on the lam.* While reading Mahler's Tenth, I realized for the first time how important silences are in music, too. So much of the score was silent, for one instrument or another. If they all sounded at once, it would be chaos.

What about sign language? Are some signs "quieter" than others?

This thought has troubled me ever since I lost my hearing. It troubled me even more when G and I started sharing more than the occasional kiss.

There are thoughts and feelings I wish I could express to her, but I don't know the signs. Sometimes I sense that she can detect what I can't say—she initiated that first kiss, after all—and maybe even understands better than I do. How, though, when those thoughts and feelings remain unsaid?

My body betrays me, I usually end up deciding. Learning

to speak a new way doesn't unlearn a very old way, one that predates all other languages. Is this something that all speakers of sign language must grapple with? Body language is simultaneously silent and more honest, for anyone who can interpret it.

Which leads me to the hospital. When no one hears, perhaps it's not simply that no one listens, but that some signs are too silent to be understood, even for those trying with all their might.

Why are you here, G? What's going on?

No phones. You promised.

What aren't you telling me?

You wouldn't understand.

I might.

You just wouldn't. But I'm glad you're here. It means more than I can say.

Can or will?

Can. Now quit with the phone before the nurses kick you out. They think you're my boyfriend, or you wouldn't be allowed in at all.

Does that mean I am your boyfriend?

Let's not have that conversation right now.

But if I'm your boyfriend, I have privileges.

Maybe. It would be more romantic, though, if you waited until they took the drip out.

I mean, you should talk to me.

What if I don't want to?

Why don't you want to?

Do I have to want to?

No, but isn't that why you asked me to come?

No.

So why?

G?

Why?

SUBAQUEOUS STUDIOS

October 7

The closest thing I found to music in the month after losing my hearing was not the gut-thumping vibrations of a band in full grind, the inspired ink-scratchings of Mahler on the page, or frenetically edited music videos on YouTube. It was the lights in Dad's studio.

Dad's house is unlike any other I know. When he and Mum split, he bought a place way out in the northeast foothills, a sprawling wedding-cake mansion that wouldn't look out of place in a soap opera. There's little yard to speak of; what there is contains nothing but gravel and apparently immortal cactus. He lives alone, apart from the odd traveling musician or roadie from the old days who might bunk down in one of the spare rooms after a bender, or maybe an infrequent, ill-advised girlfriend attempting to change his ways. None of them last long. Maeve and I never stay over much either, which seems to suit both Mum and Dad. He is there for us if we need him, but he avoids our everyday lives out of a mix of respect, awkwardness, and fear — all focused on Mum, not me and Maeve, we quickly worked out.

The first thing Dad did on taking ownership of the house was to gut the upper floor and turn it into a soundproofed recording studio. It would have been easier, and possibly cheaper, to erect an entirely new house, but he's lazy that way. He'd rather modify what already exists than conceive and build from scratch — a principle he applies to his professional life and friendships as well as his home. I'm not aware that he ever started a band or wrote an entirely original song in his life. But he's a good producer, co-writer, and bandmate, I'm told, and he's a real icebreaker at parties. As long as he doesn't have to throw one.

Even before he gave me the guitar, I used to like hanging out at the studio. It's very sci-fi, with a sweeping digital mixing desk, several flatscreens, and multiple racks of synths. The air tastes of electricity and hums with potential, like the weather before a thunderstorm. Everything is linked and has a light that shines or winks with its own color, calmly and quietly marking time.

Dad calls it "the cave," and that's exactly how it feels to me. It reminds me of our last family holiday, when we went to Waitomo in New Zealand and saw the glowworms, tiny insects who dangle from threads with their shining arses on display. In Dad's cave, as in the cave of my memory, I feel cool, calm, and full of wonder.

For Dad, the cave triggers memories of scuba gear and

bioluminescent deep-sea fish, hence the official name of the business: Subaqueous Studios. He bills himself as a "forensic synthologist" and has quite a tidy operation going in creating backing tapes for bands who've lost the ability to recreate the sounds that made them famous decades ago. I won't name names, but there are quite a few of them. You'd be surprised how hard it is to identify what made a past hit sound the way it did. Sometimes it's the right drum machine. Sometimes it's a particular preset. More often than not, it's a combination of instruments and effects that hits the memory centers of old folks' brains and makes them want to dance like it's 1988.

The work is fiddly and exacting, and really, Dad's not well compensated for the hours he puts in. Or the material investment: occasionally the sound can only be perfected by, say, purchasing a Yamaha DX1 from a collector in Fairbanks and then spending a week trying to get the wretched thing to work. His collection of synths from the eighties is one of the best in Australia.

Often, I'll find him sitting in the dark, watching the lights, or maybe letting the lights watch him. I'll sit next to him, even though I can't hear what he's hearing anymore. There's the hum of cooling fans through my fingertips, the lights, the waveforms, and his balding head nodding along in time.

Not that night, though, when I asked Mum to drop me off after walking out on Sandra. He was out somewhere, doing his own thing. I thought about texting him, but what would be the point? It was not as though there was any meaningful way to talk about what happened. How do you turn a silent scream into words?

So I just picked a backing track at random and cranked up the volume. Even if I couldn't hear it anymore, I could watch the lights and imagine the sounds of his latest brand-new imitation.

TEAR TRACKS

December 29

A proper boyfriend would respect my feelings.

I'd be happy to if I knew what they were.

I just don't feel like talking right now. Is that clear enough for you?

Okay, sure. Can *I* talk instead?

No. Please. Just

just

be

quiet

it's so loud in here

all the fucken time.

Dad came home eventually, long after dark, and found me hunched in a corner, the same track looping unheard for the hundredth time. I guess that was why he didn't look surprised. The volume was cranked up so high he probably heard it two blocks away. He nodded hello and took his seat and went back to work.

I had expected no more. The trouble with Dad is that he's great with music but terrible at pretty much anything else. Vacations, for instance. Proper vacations, I mean, not ones he can write off on his taxes because he's mixing or touring while he's in town. It's entirely possible he spent one day in his life voluntarily doing nothing, but if so, he never did it again. Being married, ditto.

Then there's shopping. Cooking. Gardening. Housekeeping. Bookkeeping. Beekeeping. (Keeping of any kind.) Driving (including golf). Parenting. And so on.

Maybe I'm being too hard on him. He hasn't been a bad father since he and Mum separated. He made sure we had keys for his place as soon as that was okay with Mum. He tops up our mobiles and provides impromptu junk food feasts. He buys us presents whenever he sees something *just right*, which makes up for getting nothing from him on birthdays and Christmas most years. He has a keen eye for things that might interest us —or maybe it's just that he gets to see us from a different and occasionally revealing perspective, compared to Mum, who has us in close focus all the time.

Maeve, like Mum, is good with numbers, so Dad has been paying her to look after his accounts since she was thirteen. She's now thinking about studying economics at uni, which never would have happened if Mum had been pushing her. Me, he got into playing music and was soon trading pocket money for rhythm or lead on jingles and demo tracks. Still does: there are ways to navigate around a studio without hearing. I learned only recently that this is how he's undercut other studios around town: by exploiting the natural talents of his kids. *Don't tell Mum* should be tattooed across his back, where she'll never see it.

He seems to understand, though, when silence is what's easiest for me.

Like when he came home to find me huddled in a studio listening to music I couldn't hear, with tear tracks down my face and a damp patch on my T-shirt.

Listen.

I recognize the documents G hands to me, even though I've never seen those specific pages before. I've seen lots just like them. They're notes from her specialists about her tinnitus.

> . . . *not a disease but a symptom that can result from one or more underlying causes . . . often but not exclusively associated with head injury . . . further neurological and cognitive testing required to determine long-term prognosis . . .*

There's such a familiar rhythm and timbre to them that if my concentration blurs, I might be reading notes about my own condition. The only difference is that she has more of them than I do. A thicker pile.

I flick through to the end.

. . . no guarantee that treatment will subdue all abnormal hyperactivity and restore the auditory cortex . . .

I read the signature at the bottom of the letter twice before realizing that it is a name I know. Prameela Verma, the sidekick who helped Selwyn Floyd determine what happened to my hearing. I feel an irrational, unreasonable flash of jealousy. Prameela never gave *me* a letter. Maybe because she had nothing to say.

Skimming back a page, I read more closely.

. . . cannot promise that a reliable intervention exists, but treatments are available that might reduce the severity for people with conditions like . . .

Certain words pop in my mind like firecrackers. *But. Treatments. Are available.*

My hands fall into my lap. G isn't looking at me, and she shakes her head when I wave the pages to attract her attention.

"This why you're here, for treatment? You're going to get better?" I say, even though neither of us can hear me speaking. I have to say *something* to let out what I'm feeling. "That's fantastic!"

She's in a private room, a sterile rectangle that smells of linoleum, plastic, and metal. There's a chair next to the bed, but I've been sitting on the edge of the mattress, as close to her as I can get without touching. Someone steps into my peripheral vision, a woman in casual clothes who looks a lot like G but older—*grandmother* is my immediate thought. The rinse in her hair is almost the same shade as G's faded purple. She's looking at me in obvious puzzlement.

I stand up, feeling awkward.

G snaps her fingers to get Grandma's attention and begins scribbling in a notepad by her bed. Grandma's eyesight isn't very good, I guess, because G's writing is big enough for me to read.

It isn't an introduction.

What did he just say?

Grandma hesitates, then checks me out again. She says something to me, and I point at my right ear and shake my head. She understands immediately and takes the pad from G's outstretched hand. In a precise cursive, she writes word for word what I said as she walked into the room. The last bit, anyway.

What happens next surprises all three of us equally, I think.

G bursts into tears.

THE MEAT FORKS

October 7

It's maddening, not being able to hear. My work with Dad, say, not really knowing what I'm playing. I'm completely reliant on him to tell me if I'm doing it right. If he's paying me for a particular kind of tone or style to match something he can only describe with words, those words aren't always sufficient. There's been the odd "What do you mean, again? That was genius!" but really it's all the same to me.

Professor Dorn told us in winter school that there's a brilliant liberation in playing with sound that is regarded by most as unmusical. How much more liberated am I, then, for playing with notes that have no sound at all?

Yeah, right. "Free Bird," that's me.

Once, not long after my stroke, Dad put on two pairs of noise-reducing headphones, in-ear and over-ear, one on top of the other, to see what the world had become for me.

Weird, he tapped out on one of his screens as we sat in silence, neither of us able to hear the racket filling the studio.

Some notes make my trouser legs flap, while others I can

feel in my shirt. Or my arm hairs. Or in my gut. Resonant frequencies, I suppose.

I had noticed that too. Different parts of us vibrate at different rates, so they pick up different tones. It's like having many different ears all over your body, each designed to hear a single note. That's how Evelyn Glennie "hears" the music she performs. Which is weird enough.

Trust Dad to give it a further spin.

We're tuning forks . . . tuning forks made of meat! There's a band name in that. The Meat Forks?

"A bit close to the Meatfuckers," I told him when he took his headphones off.

They're a thing? Jesus. I was born in the wrong century.

That was a joke. Dad claims that the name of his band, Contact, refers to sexual touching, and is a very toned-down version of another name he won't reveal to me. Sometimes it feels as if the only difference between parents and children is timing, but saying so would be a heresy for both generations.

Dad and I understand each other in a way that Mum doesn't, which isn't to say that he gets me better than she does, or is a better parent than she is, or anything like that. Having options is good, is all, when you really need them.

At least he doesn't mind me speaking when I should be signing like a good deaf boy, when I have so much to say.

Grandma and I freeze, she clearly wondering along with me if physical comfort is something G would ever want. I'd know what to do if Maeve or Mum or even Sad Alan or Roo was the one crying, but I've never met someone so tangled and knotted up as G. And yet, in her way, so sure of herself. Underneath those knots is a sword that could cut her free anytime she wants. I have to respect her decision not to.

I am wary of the sharpness of that sword, too.

The frozen instant shatters when Grandma and I move at the same time, she to take G's hand, me to put my left arm around her shoulders. She folds into me and tightly squeezes the old lady's hand. *Whew,* I think. *We got it right.*

Grandma and I glance at each other over G's head, united by that thought. "I'm Simon," I tell her. "I don't know what I did wrong."

She shakes her head as though to absolve me of responsibility. *It wasn't you,* she seems to be saying without words. But what else could it be? If G's tinnitus can be treated, why isn't she happy?

Maybe I'm slow. Maybe I'm just overwhelmed by so much information coming at me all at once. Mum tells me I'm smart, but in moments like these, I feel as dense as lead.

Until suddenly the fog parts and I start to get it.

G's long silence in recent days. Her call to come to the hospital. Her request for me to stop talking. And now, tears.

She isn't about to receive treatment. She's already had it.

And it hasn't worked.

so loud in here

all the fucken time

Fantastic, I told her. Like an idiot.

A nurse appears in the doorway and says something to Grandma, who nods without turning. The nurse inspects G from across the room, the lingering, practiced look of a health care professional, then goes away again.

G has stopped crying, but no one moves. Two of us are waiting for the other to signal what she wants. No signal comes. Part of me loosens a little then: G already has what she wants. Comfort. Support. Love.

And above all, silence. On the outside, anyway.

CONE OF SILENCE

December 29

I have a folder of photos on my phone that I use when I want to communicate with someone who can't hear, or in circumstances when I'm unsure of my ability to use my voice, such as cinemas. Am I whispering or shouting? Beats me. That's when my phone comes into play.

The folder contains photos of things I need regularly, like popcorn in the cinema scenario. It also contains screenshots of common words and phrases. Sometimes holding up a note saying *I can't hear you* is less confusing for hearing people—which is not to say that they're stupid. I would've been confused too, before. It's not something I ever consciously noted, that some deaf people can talk just fine.

Also, well, they say a picture is worth a thousand words, and that certainly applies for emotions. Dad and I have developed a shorthand for emotional exchanges, something he and I were never particularly good at even before. He's much more comfortable talking about music than feelings.

It started when I came out of hospital. He sent me a text, asking me what I'd thought of the Mahler.

I responded with a photo from the internet of <eating a giant burger>. That was the search phrase I used to capture how having that score had made me feel. Like my greedy, music-deprived neurons had woken up on realizing that starvation wasn't their only option.

He responded with <lots of thumbs up>, and we've maintained the practice since.

In the hospital, after a respectful pause, I reach for my phone and type one-handed.

<cone of silence>

The first result is an image from an old TV show. It'll do. I show it to G, and she takes the phone from me. We're so close I can practically feel the cogs in her brain whirring. She doesn't need to work hard to interpret the image. She can see the search terms right above it. She knows I'm saying without words that what happens in the hospital stays in the hospital.

G scrolls down the page past the images from the old show and selects one of a man with his head up his own arse. She shows that to me, and I know she's feeling better.

Grandma understands too. She lets go of G's hand and signs something too fast for me to understand, so she scribbles a note instead.

Hello, Simon. I'm George's Aunty Lou.

"It's nice to meet you," I say to her, because Mum hammered politeness into me along with respect for numbers. Three's a crowd, and Aunty Lou obviously doesn't know anything about me. She just sees a tall, skinny, long-haired, pierced and tattooed stranger alone in a hospital room with her niece.

"Should I be here?" I ask her, feeling a powerful urge to run. "I can leave if you want."

Aunty Lou glances down at G, and G senses that I've said something out loud. She looks up at me and mouths, *What?*

I take my arm from around her shoulders and point to the door, keeping the question in my posture. The awkwardness of the moment is only amplified by our inability to talk to each other using our voices. Every stage of this conversation buries me deeper in my natural shyness.

G rolls her eyes and says something to Aunty Lou, while at the same time waving her hands in a rough approximation of the sign for Auslan. I guess she's talking about how we met at deaf class. The three of us have separated a bit so we can see each other more clearly. I catch myself staring at G's mouth and feel self-conscious with Aunty Lou there, but what else can I do? I'm not in the least bit interested in kissing those lips right now. They are simply my best bet at trying to work out what else she's telling her aunt.

I don't see any mouth shapes that might be *boyfriend*, so I figure I best not take anything for granted.

G presses my phone onto Aunty Lou, and I glimpse the screen of the dictation app we use. Aunty Lou looks uncertain, but G closes her eyes and sinks back into the bed, leaving us to it. We have no choice, really.

This is a bit awkward, Aunty Lou says into the phone, holding it like it might bite her, which is good because that way I can see the screen.

"Yes. I'm sorry. I can go if she wants me to."

No, she wants you to stay. She wants me to tell you the way things are.

My heart sinks a little. Am I being dumped already, via old lady?

Thankfully my hurt confusion is short-lived.

Not with you and her, with me and her. George is my niece, but she lives with me. She has since she was a small girl. Her parents . . . they weren't responsible people. I never knew all the places they traveled to, or how they paid for it. Sometimes they took George with them, but usually they left her with me. I wasn't married, have never been invested in that sort of thing, and work understood. I'm a primary school teacher. George's parents came and went, and gradually the trips got longer and the visits shorter. One day they didn't come back.

"Did they die?" I ask her, gripped by this unsuspected tragedy.

No. I think they just . . . lost interest in us. Which is worse, perhaps. But more honest. George remembers them less and less clearly as time goes on. I keep hoping she'll forget entirely, but even if she does, I don't think the wound will ever heal. You should know that she has abandonment issues, if you don't already.

"Funny way of showing it," I tell her.

Oh, not really. It's safer to get out before she's thrown out —that's how she copes. She's run away so many times I've lost count, and she'll push you away before you have the chance to do the same back to her. You've seen that?

I'm nodding.

Then I'm glad you're still here, she tells me. George needs someone more than she lets on. Next time she might not be so lucky.

"Next time?" I ask her, because Aunty Lou seems to have aged ten years in a moment.

If George really doesn't want to come back, she won't. She's like her parents that way. It's only because she's not sure, I think, that she's still with us at all.

And that's when I really do get it.

G isn't in hospital because of a treatment that failed. She's in hospital because she tried to kill the noise in her head the only way she had left.

U-N-F-A-I-R

October 7

Dad and I didn't talk in the underwater cave the night I walked out on Sandra, but having him around was definitely more comforting than being on my own. Suddenly I was four again, and rituals like Ghost Spray and the presence of a parent made all the difference. So what if the world was a shitty, terrible place? Dad was with me. Everything was going to be okay.

Around midnight, I fell asleep right where I was, head dropping to my knees first, then my whole body tipping over into a fetal position, which is how I woke an unknown time later at the insistent shaking of my shoulder.

A bony hand radiated anger, like something out of my childhood wardrobe nightmare, but I wasn't dreaming. This was real.

Uh-oh, I thought, blinking up into a bright glare. The studio lights were on, as they never normally were. There were stains on the carpet that didn't bear close examination.

Bending over me, face in shadow, was Mum.

Seeing my eyes flicker open, she squatted down in front of

me and began to sign with such fury I'm amazed the air between us didn't burst into flames.

You—me—home—now.

"No," I said, and she slapped me. *Slapped* me, right across the face. Not hard, but the sting was startling. She had never done anything like that before.

Before I had a chance to recover, she clapped her hands in front of my nose. I jerked backwards and banged my head against the skirting board.

Rubbing my head, I sat up. "What are you doing? Get away from me!"

She clapped again, then made the sign for *Auslan*. Then she pointed at her ears and shook her head.

The message was clear. *Sign, or I'm not going to listen to you.*

"You can't just stop hearing—"

She shoved me and made the *Auslan* sign again, before emphasizing her point.

You—talk—me—okay. I—talk—you—how? U-N-F-A-I-R.

Mum's finger-spelling was slow but clear. She had obviously been practicing. I glanced over her shoulder at Dad, who was standing with his hips against the mixing desk. He shrugged helplessly. Obviously, he wasn't going to take sides. He never does. Not against Mum.

I pulled my phone from my pocket, intending to offer her the dictation app, and saw a dozen missed calls and texts on the lock screen. So that was why she was so mad.

Suddenly weary, I slumped back against the wall and put my hands over my eyes. Mum batted them away, thinking I was trying to block her out, but that wasn't my intention. Not specifically. It was the whole world I wanted to turn my back on, but I took her point. Closing your eyes is rude when someone's trying to talk to you.

I lowered my hands and forced myself to use them as we had been taught in deaf class. I was very rusty.

U-N-F-A-I-R—you? I—want—not—deaf!

Putting on the limited vocab and grammar I had learned was like accepting a straitjacket.

Mum placed one hand on her chest and nodded, tears flooding her eyes.

Sorry—B-U-T—you—A-R-E—deaf.

I—know!

She shushed me with a wave of one hand. She wasn't finished.

Me—mother—deaf—son. Me—learn—Auslan. You—

She poked me in the chest.

You—not—S-T-U-P-I-D—or—L-A-Z-Y. You—A-F-R-E-I-D?

I felt vengefully pleased that she made mistakes with her finger-spelling.

T-I-R-E-D.

She nodded.

Come—sleep—home.

No. T-I-R-E-D—everything. Want—F-O-R-B-E-T.

She frowned. Instant karma. I tried that word again.

F-O-R-G-E-T.

Nodding, she folded her hands in mine and pressed them to her forehead, like she wanted to absorb my words directly into her brain—which she *could* have done if she'd only let me speak. That's what the human voice is for, after all.

And that's what Auslan is for too, I knew. But practice required energy, and I was burning up enough of that just adapting to not having music, or a life, or even Shari, apparently . . .

I wondered what would happen if I really did drop out of everything for six months or even a year, however long it would take to learn what I needed to learn and become whoever I needed to become. A deaf person. A stranger.

Would that stranger recognize the old me? Would I lose my entire self along with those final notes of life's great symphony?

Mum shook her head, and for a second I wondered if I had spoken aloud. I hadn't. She had her own questions, I realized, her own anxieties. Her son couldn't hear. That changed things for her, too. It had to. I was never going to hear the school bell ring again or the buzzer going off to tell me to take something out of the oven. I was never going to hear someone cry out in pain if they stubbed their toe. I was never going to hear her telling me to pick up my shoes or know if she was on the other end of a phone call. All small things, but that didn't mean they weren't important. Life is an accumulation of small things, adding up to a ziggurat that with a big enough shove can be toppled.

I knew all this. I was living it. But that didn't mean I had to like it.

"So I can't stay here?"

Mum looked up, and her eyes were bloodshot. She shook her head. The rule was that Maeve and I had to give her twenty-four hours' notice if we were going to be at Dad's, and I guess she was sticking to that in the face of things she couldn't control, life's unquantifiable twists.

"Let's go, then."

I stood and brushed past her, scooping down to pick up my backpack where it slouched by the door. Dad reached out to touch my shoulder as I went by, but I didn't say anything to him. I felt betrayed.

Mum has never had a key to Dad's house; he must have let her in. So much for being safe there.

The car was out front, windows lightly misted from the cool night air. I leaned against it, unable to get in. Mum didn't follow immediately. Presumably she was laying down the law to Dad in my absence, although it wouldn't have made much difference if I was there. I wouldn't have overheard a thing.

I thought about running off into the night, but only for a fleeting moment. Defiance took energy too. I wasn't like Maeve, who often threatened to live on the streets if she didn't get her way. Her arguments with Mum last for days sometimes, but she's still at home. I'm not sure that isn't also an act of revenge.

Mum appeared and unlocked the car. That is, the lights flashed, but I couldn't hear the *bip-bip,* of course. I got inside and buckled the seat belt, keeping my backpack on my lap as though I could still bolt at any moment. She got in behind the wheel. Her red Civic rocked and settled, then came alive with an inaudible cough. The seat vibrated under me as Mum pulled away from the curb, driving us steadily through the dark streets toward home.

We weren't done, though. Just because her hands were on the steering wheel and therefore she couldn't talk to me, that didn't mean I had to be silent.

"I can't remember the first album I ever heard," I told her, "but the first I remember loving was Black Sabbath's *Paranoid*. Dad used to play it in the car when he picked me up from day-care. Maeve and I would sit in the back and sing along to 'Iron Man,' making up the words as we went. I didn't realize that it wasn't actually about *Iron Man* the movie until years later, but that only makes me love it more. Music that hides its message is the best kind—that's what Professor Dorn says, and I think she's right."

I could have been doing nothing more than working my jaw and tongue muscles, for all Mum reacted, apart from a slight tightness around her eyes, so I kept going. From first favorite album to the first I ever owned, then to the first I ever bought. The first band I ever followed. The best song they ever wrote. Best albums ever. Best album openers ever. Best one-hit wonders.

I was onto best guitar solos by the time we pulled into our driveway, and I was pretty sure she was going to slap me again. My cheek still felt tender from the first time, although that was probably just the memory of it, not an authentic sensation. I'm pretty sure too that my speech to her was retaliation for her hitting me, but it might also have been a form of catharsis

—vomiting up a clotted mass of things that would never matter to me again. The detritus of my hearing life. All the crap that Sandra had wanted me to say.

And she bore it, like I guess she had to. She's my mother.

The car rattled to a halt and she sat still for a moment, keys in hand, looking like she wanted to sign something, but then she just got out and went inside.

I stayed in the passenger seat, feeling nothing but shame.

NERVE STIMULATION

December 29

A composer writes notes on a page in an attempt to capture the music they hear in their head, knowing full well that it will change when played, filtered through the perceptions of conductor, performer, and audience.

From the age of sixteen, I wrote tattoos into my skin in an attempt to capture my identity, completely ignorant of the possibility that I might change in any substantial way. How could I have known that one day these marks would bring me pain far worse than the original needle had?

Back of my right shin: a bass clef.

Inside my right wrist: three barred semiquavers.

Back of my left hand: a key signature, C-sharp major.

Above my left nipple: a time signature, 7/8 (inked a week after I lost my virginity to Cass Bonnici, who came out as a lesbian the next day).

Along the inside of my left arm: an empty stave curving like a banner in the wind.

On the back of my neck: the chord progression from Slipknot's "Psychosocial."

At the time of my stroke I was considering a seventh tattoo for my eighteenth birthday, a power chord written in tablature, but afterwards my heart wasn't in it. How does one write one's identity when one no longer knows what it is?

Sudden deafness isn't a disease with a fatality rate . . .

In the middle of October, Deaf Solutions assigned me another counselor, who picked up where we had left off, talking entirely via the cloud. An older Asian guy, he too explored the depths of my unhappiness by means of platitudes, with occasional all caps.

. . . UNLESS you factor in suicide.

After the maddening Sandra Mack, I found his bullshit refreshingly blunt. He could be funny, too. His name was Killian Ollerenshaw, which he immediately admitted was too much of a handful to sign. Instead, people called him KO.

Like that old song: "Total KO! To-kyo Go!" You know it?

Oh yeah.

What was the band? Context?

Contact.

THAT'S RIGHT! I used to have their poster on my bedroom wall. That probably seems totally uncool now.

So then I had to confess about Dad, and then Mum, and then everything else. If it was a deliberate ploy, much respect.

But I reckon it was just a lucky accident. For him, I mean. I didn't really want to talk about what had happened in the previous days. I'd had enough time to realize I was being selfish for expecting everyone around me, who had battles of their own to get on with, to stand about waving banners for me. (No point blowing trumpets.)

It's hard not to be selfish, though, when you're trapped behind the veil of silence. No — a one-way mirror, because I can communicate easily enough with hearing people. It's the other way that's hard. When you're give, give, give all the time, is it wrong to expect something in return? Wasn't I permitted to be a shit at least part-time?

. . . suicide.

Standing by G's bed at the end of the year, KO's stark pronouncement comes back to me. G is undergoing some kind of treatment, a cure for the noise that plagues her, drowning out the world. But it doesn't work, and . . .

If she really doesn't want to come back, Aunty Lou said. She wasn't talking about going on vacation.

I know I'm being selfish again, trying to find a way to process what's happening to G through the filter of my own experiences, but how else am I supposed to do it?

By trying on one of G's filters. That's the straw I clutch at. I still have the sheaf of letters in my hand, and I begin to read them more closely. The first thing I see is an acronym, VNS. Then another, TR-MDD. The language is technical and hard to follow. I feel like I'm reading something in French or Italian: the letters are the same, but the words make no sense to me. Something about nerves and electrical signals. Implants and computer-aided therapy. Neuromodulators and transmitters.

If I squint, I could almost be reading a manual for one of Dad's synths.

Which is a stupid, stupid thought. G doesn't have a manual, and neither does her condition. I'm chasing something that doesn't exist. Is it any wonder that the words in front of me are utterly removed from their meaning?

Aunty Lou is trying to tell me something. I look up from the page, and she hands me a note.

Take it. Read it. We have another copy.

Her offer feels like a dismissal, but maybe I'm ready to go now. Not understanding makes me an outsider, and while G's eyes are closed, I can't ask her questions.

But am I offering silent support just by being here? What message would I send if I left now?

I sit in the visitor's chair. My hands are shaking. I don't really see the words on the pages anymore. My insides are an eel that's squeezing tighter with every breath. Part of me needs to flee, but I know I have to stay. I *want* to stay. I want to know how to make a difference.

Phrases like this don't help: *Cortical Map Plasticity as a Function of Vagus Nerve Stimulation*.

All I see are three potential song titles.

• • •

Take a word and its meaning. Separate the two—and you're left with noise. But I don't believe in "noise." If every sound is musical, then every word has meaning, even if it's not the one intended.

. . . suicide.

The very thought of what G has done scares me shitless.

Perhaps it's this that gives me a flash of inspiration.

According to the notes G handed me, she has a chip in her head now. That's the reason for the new scar on her neck that I noticed at uni. It isn't a cochlear implant, though. A cochlear implant processes sound and feeds it directly into the nervous system of your inner ear. Not just the sound of the world around you: you can connect your phone to your implant and hear things that were never real. No one else can hear these sounds but you.

That's the germ of my new thought, and the hospital room grays out around me as I pursue it, imagining a performance piece that never even once exists as sound. It would start as information in a computer, say, then that information would be fed wirelessly into a hall full of people with cochlear implants, so they would all hear music appearing out of apparent silence. Ghost tunes over Wi-Fi. Even better than a silent disco.

Problems are immediately apparent, some of them solvable. People who don't have implants can wear earbuds, which wouldn't sound exactly the same, but some variability has to be permissible. No musical experience is identical to any other, even if you're listening to the same song on repeat. Like that river we can never cross twice.

Still, expensive, and it relies on hearing *something* in the brain. This is a stunt that wouldn't work on someone like me, missing the crucial part that hears.

But the possibility has my mind turning over idea after idea, sensing that I'm getting closer to something even better. Being selfish again, hiding from the problem at hand. Later, I will be guilt stricken. For now, though, in the hospital, the chain of thought pulls me irresistibly onwards.

Computers are boring to watch. Why not a band playing electronic instruments? That wouldn't work so well with Blackmod, unless we took up keytars and electric drums, which I know Roo or Sad Alan wouldn't do. Still, let's imagine.

If the synths aren't plugged in, no one's missing out on anything.

Or what if they *are* plugged in, but the faders on the mixing desk are down and the amps aren't turned up?

Or everything's working as normal, but the audience is wearing noise-reducing headphones?

No, too expensive, again—and all it takes is for someone to remove the headphones to ruin the effect.

I've hit this roadblock before. The difficulty of creating audible music that isn't audible to anyone is very apparent to me.

Only . . . my brain is really beginning to fizz now . . . the music doesn't have to be inaudible to *anyone*.

It just has to be inaudible to *the audience*.

In that moment, the first work of impossible music is born.

Its existence is a comfort in a world that until now has offered no comfort at all.

DEAF AND DUMB

October 7

When I first met KO, my new counselor, he wanted to know why I'd walked out on his predecessor. He had Sandra Mack's side of the story, of course, and he wanted to hear mine. That was going to require me to fess up about my darker emotions and feeling patronized and being an arse to Mum afterwards, and I told him that would take too long to type out.

I'm in no hurry, he said. Better that than keeping it bottled up inside you.

So I tried. I described how I'd felt sitting in the car after my prolonged spit about all the music I'd never hear again. I knew I had to apologize to Mum but didn't know how. Signing it wouldn't feel real—so little felt real anymore, except for the intensity of my anger and frustration—but saying "sorry" aloud would risk things flaring up again. Texting wasn't an option . . . was it? I decided it wasn't. But how were we going to move forward if I couldn't heal that breach? I couldn't live in the car . . . though part of me was attracted to that idea. It was safe in there. The seats were comfortable. I was alone.

When I closed my eyes and settled back, my pulse slowed, my muscles slackened—

Thump thump thump—

I felt rather than heard a fist pounding on the roof of the car. My eyes snapped open, then slammed shut as the overhead light blasted on. Someone was getting in behind the wheel. Rough hands pushed a hard-edged oblong into my stomach. I had to look, even though my eyes were still adjusting.

It was Maeve and her trusty whiteboard. She'd written three words in red and underlined them four times in black.

Deaf and dumb.

I scowled at the message. "I can talk just fine," I told her, but I knew what she was really saying. "And I'm not stupid."

Her nonverbal language was almost as easy to read as the words on her whiteboard.

You're sure acting stupid. Like running to Dad's was ever going to help. If anything, it makes it worse. Mum is inside listening to that boring music of hers, you know. She's on her second repeat.

"I'll come in when I'm ready."

Two hands palm up in the air. A gesture, not a sign: *When will that be?*

"What do you care?"

On the whiteboard, she wrote, *You're my brother, you asshole. Come inside.*

"I'm surprised you haven't already moved into my room."

A single raised eyebrow, a tilt of the head. *Oh, believe me, I'm tempted.*

I sighed, wishing I could ask her what I should do about Mum. But we didn't have that kind of relationship. She thought I was a loser, and I thought she was annoying. For all that we were less than a year apart and our paths often intersected, the orbits we followed were way out of alignment. Chalk and cheese, math and music—we had nothing in common except the house we lived in.

She performed some substantial editing on the board.

brother + stroke = pain in the ass

Well, we agreed on that. I hated having brain damage, and she hated me having brain damage. All this drama made life difficult for her too, although it was hard to remember that, sometimes.

"Look at the upside," I said, and she tilted her head the other way, *WTF?*

"You can play that K-pop shit all you want now, and I don't have to listen to it."

Her eyebrows came up. *Yeah, see?* She erased the board with one sweep of her sleeve and tugged at my arm. *Coming?*

"I will if you tell Mum I'm sorry first."

She looked at me through lowered brows and meaningfully shook her head. *That's on you, sonny.*

Then she was moving, and, almost as though I had no

volition, so was I. Out of the car, across the yard, through the back door, into the kitchen. Mum was there, nursing a mug of cocoa and a wary look. I signed *Sorry* twice, the word feeling awkward in my hand but sincerely meant, and she nodded, not without sympathy. Nothing was resolved, but we had moved on. That was enough.

I went to my room and erased the iTunes folder on my laptop. Dumb to keep it, and I felt an act of contrition was required. Upside, I told myself: more room for porn.

Finding an upside to losing music has been hard for me. Here's another one: no more worries about earbuds breaking or getting lost.

Mostly it was shit, though, not being able to hear, and for so many reasons I could have listed them all day. Maeve is always telling me when my shoes are squeaking or I'm making other noises I'm not aware of. The "groaning ghost," she calls me sometimes, when I'm humming along to head music without realizing. The habit is ingrained.

And speaking of porn, masturbating is so nerve-racking I'd almost rather not try. Is there someone outside my room? Will they walk in and catch me at it? Having a younger sister in the house automatically makes locks fifty percent less reliable.

Sudden deafness takes something already fraught with potential disaster and makes it seem utterly impossible. Being in general, I mean, not just wanking.

In the silence of my world, it's all too easy to fixate on my issues and forget about everyone else's. Hence, I am less likely to die by my own hand than by crossing the road and not hearing the car speeding around a corner.

Was G fixating too, in the noise of her world? Or did she already feel drowned out? Erased?

She tried to kill herself. She failed. Then she called me. And now I tell myself to think about the future. There has to be one, or why would I be here?

KO asked whether my breakup with Shari and the argument with Mum changed the way I felt about myself or my situation. He obviously wanted me to say yes, and that is indeed what I told him—because it was true, and because I had learned to choose my battles. The situation I was in impacted on those around me. My parents and sibling had a deaf member of the family now, which in some ways seemed as confronting as if I'd become a paraplegic. Only, instead of ramps, we had to build bridges—bridges spanning the gulf of misunderstanding that lay between us.

Finding a way to do that was the hard thing. Silence meant as much as the spoken word to me, as far as my brain was concerned. Close my mouth, open it . . . withdraw, unburden . . . I might as well have flapped my jaw up and down like a ventriloquist's dummy.

Time, KO tapped into our shared file in the cloud.

That's the cure for what ails you. I'm not talking about

deafness, although it's good you can use that word now. (Maybe one day you'll even spell it with a capital D.) I mean your sense of being alone and forgotten by a world that's moved on without you. Forget the songs you'll never hear again—what about the new music you'll never hear AT ALL? What about the new ringtones on the next iPhone? What about—

Yeah, I get it.

I think you're starting to. You imagine yourself staring into a world empty of sound, and you see only blankness. It takes time to see that it's just as full as it ever was. Breakups make you feel the same way, which is why I think these two crises have come together. I promise you'll find someone else, and I also promise you'll find a way to be Deaf, too. Your own way.

How? What does that even mean?

Perhaps it would help to ask what it was about music that you liked. If it's rhythm and structure, maybe dance could be a substitute. There are Deaf dancers. If it's the social aspect, the drinking—drugs, even—

I'm not interested in substitutes. Music is my drug. Every bit of it.

Well, we'll just have to find you another drug. (DON'T tell anyone I said that.) Does it help to know that there are other people out there looking too?

I wondered then how many people he saw every day. Single figures? Double? But he wouldn't tell me.

No one follows the same path, Simon. Lots of people are lost. You're not alone.

Great, I wanted to say, *and I bet Gustav Mahler had company too.*

SOMETHING QUIET

December 29

In the hospital, I come back to that wordless shrug—"How?" —and a message from G that had been waiting for me on Christmas morning, a grim response to my description of the stroke, or so I guessed at the time.

Remember that accident I told you about? The roller derby? My wrists? I have a vivid memory of hitting the ground and the whistle the ref blew, but it's a blur after that, apart from the pain. There was swearing. Quite a lot of swearing, I suspect. When the ambulance arrived, they loaded me up with seriously awesome painkillers. The next thing I know, I'm lying in hospital with my hands in plaster and there's Aunty Lou by the bed and a doctor talking to me, but somehow I can still hear the ref's whistle that sounded as I went down. Peep-peep. Peep-peeeep. Peep-fucking-peeeeeeeeeeeeeeeeeeep.

At first I think I'm imagining it. I mean, it's not there all the time. Mostly when people are talking. I can still understand what they're saying, but it's harder to make out the words. Sometimes the whistle surprises me out of nowhere and makes me jump. I feel like an idiot, but an idiot is better than crazy, which I feel like I might be sometimes, too.

Eventually Aunty Lou notices the jumping and insomnia and she makes me go see the doctor. I tell them about the whistle, and they tell me it's all in my head —which I suppose, technically, that's what tinnitus IS, one way or another. Either the nerves are overactive or the brain is, take your pick. They say there's no physical cause they can detect and that stress could be making it worse, because I missed a bunch of school and my midyear exams didn't go as well as I hoped—so they put me on antidepressants, but that only makes the noise louder. I don't tell anyone because by then my hands are pretty much better and I'm ready to skate again, and nothing's going to stop the Diva Hammer from going back, dammit.

That's when things really went to shit.

Yeah. So. There was a second accident. That's the real reason why I don't skate anymore. I was so used to ignoring the whistle in my head that I didn't pay attention to the one I was supposed to hear in the real world. Five minutes into my first bout back, the other team's jammer stops right in front of me, and I don't notice in time. I trip over her legs and crash into the barrier so hard I knock myself clean out. Because I'm protecting my hands. I'm lucky I don't break my neck instead. I'm lucky I wake up at all.

That's what they write down for me when they realize I can't make out anything over the racket in my head that's now one hundred times more terrible than before. Random sounds on a loop, over and over, with no break, ever. Voices, snatches of music, ringtones, dogs barking. Nothing they can do about it but wait to see if it goes away—which it isn't doing. In fact, it's getting worse.

But hey, look on the bright side! At least the fucking whistle is gone.

Four days after reading that email, I look at her in the hospital bed, with her arms lying limply by her sides, and notice that her eyes are open. She is staring at me. I feel a jolt, like someone flicked a switch inside me, and I wonder if she ever properly explained the way she felt to anyone else. She must have a Sandra Mack or KO to sound off at, however uselessly. Does she hide it from them because there's no solution? Because she doesn't want Aunty Lou to worry?

Does she want me to worry?

Her eyes flicker shut, and I am locked out again.

I want her to talk. I want to ask questions. I want to know if she sent that message right before she did it, and whether I could've made a difference if I'd been online instead of watching *Love Actually* for the tenth year in a row (hard to say if it was any funnier subtitled) and digesting a giant feast with my mother and sister. I want her to tell me how she did it, because I see no bandages, no bruises, or other signs of violence, and the chart above her bed doesn't explain anything.

Absently, I note the index finger of her right hand tapping, tapping, tapping to a beat no one else can hear.

Drugs, I decide.

After everything she's been through, she'd want something quiet.

I feel like weeping.

But all I do is sit silently until G falls asleep. Then I figure my job is done, for the moment. I say good night to Aunty Lou, and she says thank you, clutching my hand briefly like she's found an ally in a dark corner.

PART FOUR

"PLASTIC MAPS"

December 29

To: Grace Dorn

From: Simon Rain

Date: December 29

Subject: Impossible Music

Hey Professor D,

I imagine it will look something like this:

"Plastic Maps"

Two people walk onto a stage where their instruments await. Everything's wired: sequencers, electronic drums, synths, etc. Each machine has a flashing light. There are no microphones. No speakers, either.

Behind the stage, a giant projector screen displays a fish-eye view of the street outside. Pedestrians, cars going by, more flashing lights. It's rush hour. People are everywhere.

The performers look at each other. One of them counts off their fingers. Lights flash faster as the music starts.

But what's this? No sound!

The hearing audience is confused for a moment. Are the performers miming? Are their instruments not plugged in? Or is the electricity of their performance vanishing down an earthed wire somewhere, never to be heard at all?

The deaf audience take it in their stride. "Plastic Maps" is silent for everyone, apparently.

It could end there, but it doesn't. As the performance progresses, people begin to notice what's happening on the screen. Passersby are responding to an invisible stimulus. They don't know where it comes from, but it's there, and it's infectious. Poppy, even. Familiar.

They react because they can hear music—the music of the performance, broadcast without announcement to the world outside. Every note the duo plays is vanishing, but at the same time it exists. Just because the audience inside can't hear it, doesn't mean it isn't real to someone.

When the piece finishes, the performers bow. They haven't heard their music either, but they have brought it into being, and it is done.

The audience will be left with the feeling of having experienced something. But was it something real, or something denied them—an absence, a theft? And ultimately, was it music?

What do you reckon?

Rain

To: Simon Rain

From: Grace Dorn

Date: December 29

Subject: Re: Impossible Music

Rain—

Promising. Press on. Two more will convince me that this is worth pursuing, not just a stunt.

RAIN PARADE

November 5

After our first post-Shari practice in October, Sad Alan, Roo, and I rehearsed for a couple of weeks before calling it quits. Blackmod still existed as an entity in the garage, but nowhere else. And that, frankly, was something of a relief. I liked playing live and missed it, but the thought of making the attempt now made me even more anxious than it had in the beginning. Everything needed to work as one to make even a halfway decent live gig. When you added a deaf lead guitarist to the many other things that could go wrong, the prospect became more terrifying than it was worth.

Which is not to say we didn't try to find a way. There was the Zappa signaling method, but that only worked if we were looking at each other and had hands or other limbs free to say "you're flat" or "you're dragging" or "wrong song, dickhead!"

Next, we tried reworking some of the arrangements so the kick drum would provide cues that I could feel rather than hear. However, concentrating on those cues led all of us to play like robots. We might as well have sacked Sad Alan and bought a drum machine.

Maybe if we'd been super-professional before I lost my hearing we might have survived the transition. But, sadly, we were just kids messing around with loud noises. Without hearing the noise, all I made was a mess.

It was hard to step back from the stage and set the two of them free, but it had to be done. For their sakes. I couldn't drag my best friends down into silence with me. And it wasn't as if we didn't still have Blackmod. We played for the three of us now, no one else.

The plug was officially pulled on my eighteenth birthday, and the guys took me out for something that felt at least partly like a commiseration, although I don't remember most of it. My hangover of the next morning is, alas, painfully clear.

Within a fortnight, Roo invited Sad Alan to join a group he'd formed some weeks earlier with two girls he knew from their part-time work at Subway. Slave Leia billed itself as post-post-punk: high-energy, kinetic, sexy, with a unified aesthetic and even the odd moment of choreography. That was Sad Alan, not the girls—Roo crossed his heart, hoped to die.

They dragged me to their opening gig, and despite the irrational jealousy I couldn't help feeling, I found it to be good, infectious fun. Jumping to the beat alongside friends and strangers was the easiest thing in the world. It felt liberating to be part of the crowd, no different from anyone else, while it lasted.

The same thing happened that always happens after gigs,

though. As people started talking, I could only nod along or shake my head and stand in a corner, hoping no one would bother me.

Hey, guy with the hair. You're Alan and Roo's friend, right?

The text came from a number my phone didn't recognize. There was no way to tell if the source was in the room or half-way across the country.

Who are you, and how did you get my number?

I have my ways.

Yeah, this is not creepy at all.

A tiny woman with short blond pigtails appeared in front of me, grinning and waving her phone. I didn't know her, but I'd just watched her performing in the band. Keyboards and vocals: I had heard neither, but my eyes had been entertained.

I'm Mia, your stalker for the evening. Wanna buy me a drink?

Mia's energy was infectious enough to punctuate my mood. We forced our way to the bar, where I used a large-print app and my file of photos to order two Coopers Pales. I was still enjoying the ability to legally drink and had finally got over the hangover of my eighteenth-slash-end-of-rock-god-career bash.

We clinked glasses. I felt the cold ringing in my finger-tips. The crowd was too loud for voice recognition, so we kept texting.

It's great to finally meet you. The boys talk about you a lot.

None of it is true, I swear.

Did you know they wrote a song about you? They weren't going to tell you, but I think it's right to own your muse. You know, in case you have a hit and your muse decides to sue.

Oh, I would. What's it called?

"Rain Parade." We played it tonight. Fourth song in.

What's the chorus?

"She's raining on my rain parade / mistaken while I play charades" . . . I didn't say it's any good.

Better than anything they've done before. Are you sure it's inspired by me?

It's about a guy who wants to break a girl's heart, but she's deaf so he has to mime it.

Deep.

Yeah, that's what I said. And swapping genders has never been done before. Did she really break your heart, whoever she was?

Kinda. You know when you probably would've broken up with someone but they got in first? It was like that.

Never happened to me. Weird, huh?

Mia leaned in close, gifting me with a wave of perfume and sweat. I thought she was about to kiss me, and maybe I would've kissed her back, but instead she put her mouth next to my ear. Her lips moved. I felt her breath against my skin. When she pulled away, her eyes were dancing. They were blue and brilliant.

You didn't hear that?

No.

Boy, you really are deaf.

She did it again, this time standing even closer, for longer, presumably going into more detail.

How about now?

Okay. Let me see if I got it right.

I returned the gesture and spoke directly into her ear. She put a hand around my waist and pressed full-length against me for as long as it took me to say seven words.

"Being deaf is not a pickup line."

Then I pulled away from her and headed for the nearest exit. Out of the corner of my eye I saw her mouth moving unintelligibly. "Thanks for the show," I called over my shoulder, but I don't know if I spoke loudly enough for her to hear. Whispering or screaming, it's all the same to me.

On the way home, I deleted her texts and blocked her number. It's not exactly flattering, being offered a pity fuck or whatever was going through her mind. Maybe she wanted to sleep with a guy she could say anything to. Or maybe she was just messing with me. I didn't know, and I told myself I didn't care. She had scratched my surface and exposed the dreadful mix of anger, anxiety, and shame that lurked beneath.

But it wasn't entirely unflattering, either, and the encounter snapped me out of the self-pitying funk that Shari and Blackmod had dropped me in.

Mum was on the couch, where she'd fallen asleep watching Netflix. I tried not to wake her, but I must've closed the door too hard or bumped into something or just breathed too heavily. She sat up, rubbed her eyes, and signed, *Fun night?*

I gave her a thumbs-up and mimed a yawn. Gestures, not signs. Neutral territory, still.

She waved as I headed to my room. There, I picked up the guitar, plugged it straight into my laptop, and recorded something fast and angry, but not too bitter. I was aiming for an old-school metal riff with plenty of energy, using effects settings I remembered from aping a Judas Priest album once. Throw in a little Satriani, and you get the idea.

Something clicked in my head as I played. Sure, I couldn't perform with Blackmod anymore, not outside the garage, but here I was playing my own music, and nothing was stopping me from doing that. I had no one to keep time with, no one else's pitch to match. It was just me, alone, and maybe that could work. All I needed was a venue that would allow a deaf guitarist to get up and play . . .

I dismissed the slightly-less-crazy thought of joining Mr. Mackereth in Rundle Mall, busking for spare change. I would feel like someone from a freak show, unable to hear if passersby were cheering or jeering, completely exposed.

But getting up in front of a literal crowd is not the only way to find an audience, and as my solo chugged to a stupendous finale, the alternative was clear in my mind.

When the last virtual echo had faded to silence (according to the indicators on my laptop), I trimmed the sound file, called it "Pain Grade," and uploaded it to the internet under the username Deafman, a nod to Steven Wilson. In the bio for Deafman, I said my goal was "to make some noise in a silent world" and that I came from Mars, "where sound doesn't work." I dedicated the recording to "Shia" (Shari + Mia) and privately hoped someone would think I meant LaBeouf. I took a blurry photo of my right ear and uploaded that for my userpic. Then I put it out on my usual social media at two a.m. on November the 5th, two months and three days after I lost my hearing.

MADDENING HINTS

December 30

There's a kind of joy in flying in the face of futility. I got that feeling from releasing "Pain Grade," and I suppose the fumes of it are sustaining me now, in the face of Professor Dorn's demand.

Two more impossible music ideas? I didn't get the first until my maybe-girlfriend tried to commit suicide . . .

Still, I put every effort into it, researching haptic music accessories, high-tech gadgets that turn the vibrations up to eleven. Some are strapped to your body like miniature subwoofers; others resemble bulletproof vests, with actuators that thump different parts of your body depending on what frequencies are being activated. That, I thought, could be cool. Mechanical meat forks.

But, again, expensive. Does every idea slam up against that brick wall?

Not all of them, I'm pleased to say. "Plastic Maps" takes something normal and simply rearranges it, so sound and performance will be separate. If I can come up with another concept like that, awesome. And then another one.

Or maybe I can skip the idea of performance entirely. Already it is slipping from my everyday thoughts as I concentrate on more arcane ways of making music. My mind is stuck on a hall full of people being thudded and buzzed by machines in time with music they can't hear . . . It's too amazing an image. I can't let go of it.

Of course, the concept of "touch" is a flexible one, just like music itself. People are incredibly empathetic: we flinch when we see someone else being hurt. Perhaps there's an idea worth exploring here? Could showing people images of instruments being hit or plucked provide a similar sensation to that of hearing them?

Or maybe I don't even need images. Light alone could be enough. Photons would "touch" everyone in the audience at the same time, without preference for either the deaf or the hearing. Music visualizers already convert sound to light shows, but the idea goes back much further than iTunes and VJs. There were "color organs" in the eighteenth century, mechanical devices that translated sound into things people could see—and while that's cool, it might mean I'll be hard pressed to come up with a novel twist.

Color organs were big fifty years ago too, as trippy as lava lamps but on a much bigger scale. I watch a bunch of old concerts on YouTube and am not particularly impressed. Too slow, too amorphous, too dim. We could do much better these days with high-powered LEDs, maybe even lasers. Or with projections of those silent GIFs that some people claim to hear?

But to what end? What would be the point? Professor Dorn is never going to give me the go-ahead for a pretty light show. At the very least, I'm going to need some *music* . . .

"Lava lamp" triggers a memory I'd rather not pursue, but I follow it in case it leads somewhere useful.

Shari's parents owned a vibrating bed. Why? I have no idea. Prior to meeting her, I didn't even know such things existed. Needless to say, we wanted to check it out. Her parents were such stay-at-homes, though (maybe because of the bed), that we didn't get the chance until after my stroke. On that day, when things weren't too tense between us, she texted to invite me over.

Buzz buzz—it's finally free!

OMG

Stop texting. Get moving!

I scoped out her driveway on approach. As promised, no sign of Shari's parents' car, a giant silver beast about as old as the very notion of a vibrating bed. She had already explained that they were at a Greek Orthodox wedding and wouldn't be back until dinnertime at the earliest. I grinned. That gave us hours to explore the possibilities.

My good mood lasted about as long as it took for her to let me in.

The freight train scooped me up and delivered me to the bedroom, where we had the same problem we always did. It's much easier to be deaf when you're alone. Being around someone you never really communicated with in the first place is a reminder of how much you took for granted, and wasted. Vibrating bed or no vibrating bed.

Afterwards, I lay sprawled on the trembling mattress while she played a version of "I Spy" by spelling out letters with her fingertip on my stomach. I correctly guessed about one word in three; maybe I would have been more successful if I'd been paying attention.

"Pillow?"

"Foot? Too easy."

"Lava lamp—really?"

My mind was mainly on the bed's vibrations. They felt much stronger when I was lying still, and maybe I was beginning to see the point of them now. I felt electrically adrift, as though I had entered Mum's favorite meditation music and become one with the very idea of sound. *Ommmmm.*

I didn't know I'd gone to sleep until Shari shook me awake. Night had fallen. Headlights were moving across the window, painting blocky white shapes on the far wall and across her face. Her mouth was moving, urgently.

Her parents were back!

We threw the sheets together as though we were in the worst sitcom ever and barely reached the living room in time to make it look like they'd caught us fooling around out there. Everyone blushed and looked awkward, but I couldn't hear what they said to her, so I didn't know until later that they'd banned me from coming over again. I just said goodbye as politely as I could and left them to it.

A better boyfriend would have stayed to share the punishment.

Lava lamps and vibrating beds.

There's something in this memory that I can't put my finger on. Something so obvious I can't see it. The hint is tantalizing and maddening. I need this idea, need it badly. I have to convince Professor Dorn that I'm getting somewhere with this, or else she won't let me into her course—and if she won't do that, then what am I supposed to do with my life?

Briefly, I consider texting Shari to see if talking to her shakes anything loose. Then sanity kicks in, and I message G instead. Perhaps a distraction will help. She's been under observation in the hospital five days now, detoxing or whatever doctors make people do when they've taken an overdose, assuming that's what she did. She must be bored out of her mind. I was in the hospital for some knee surgery when I was a kid, and every minute of those two days dragged.

Good night and good morning.

Where are you? Bring coffee.

I smile. G is back to normal, for her version of "normal."

I can be there in an hour.

Too long. I'm fading fast.

Maeve has the car, but she's due back any minute now.

Note to self: next boyfriend must have own mobile cafe.

Gotta get rid of this one first.

Is that a challenge? I accept.

A second later, my phone vibrates. It's G requesting a Skype session. She appears on the screen, pointing at her face with an *I dare you to comment* expression. She does look somewhat below par, I have to admit. Her hair is simultaneously greasy and flyaway. Her face has pink lines down one side, as if she woke up lying on a tangle of rope. Dark rings bag her eyes, almost certainly not mascara.

Still, my heart does a little thud-thud on seeing her. Silent, but present.

Wasn't that you in *The Ring*?

Dude, you're the one with long hair.

Enjoy it while it lasts: my dad is an egg.

That's not how baldness genes work.

I think?

Beats me.

Shall I come visit?

Dunno, SHALL you?

Don't hate me for my grammar.

Just bring coffee. Don't forget!

G ends the call, and I go to get ready, cheerful at the prospect of seeing her again. She may be sick, but I want to be with her, particularly when she's feeling chatty. Maybe her tinnitus isn't so bad today.

Maeve's schedules run on a plus-or-minus-half-an-hour principle. I'm practically dancing by the door, waiting to speed off through the suburbs when she gets home. Seeing my eagerness, she has fun holding the keys just out of reach and switching them from hand to hand behind her back. I don't have time for this.

I pick her up and take her bodily back outside, feeling her laughing against me until I drop her down next to the car. She hands me the keys and reaches for her phone.

What's the hurry? Hot date?

With burning cheeks, I let myself into the car. "Don't wait up," I tell her and reverse out the drive.

The sky is cloudy, threatening summer rain. I crank the window down and tie my hair back in an attempt to keep it out of my face. The hot wind just makes it feel heavier.

Being behind the wheel of a car was weird at first. There are so many audio cues when you're driving. The sound of the engine revving. The clicking of indicators. Squeaking brakes. The ancient Civic Maeve and I share has more than its fair share of quirks, and there's not an indicator light for any of them.

Then there are the other cars on the road. I can't hear horns honking or sirens approaching. More than once, I've been caught out by the latter. When you're watching everything all at once to make up for being unable to hear, it's amazingly easy to miss flashing lights weaving through the traffic behind you. Sunlight glinting off chrome is something you quickly learn to ignore because it looks like emergency vehicle lights. Same with strobing bike lights at night. Ignore all the false alarms, and eventually you'll miss a real one, just like G and her ref's whistle.

I know that some deaf drivers have extra rearview mirrors

so they can watch what's being signed in the back seat, but I can't imagine trying to follow a conversation with my eyes while behind the wheel. The thought is terrifying. I'm too busy watching the entire world at once to think about words.

Distracting habits are hard to break, though. On the way to the hospital, my phone, flopped face-up on the passenger seat, rat-a-tats its flash to let me know a text has arrived. Another one quickly follows. Then another.

I glance down at it to read the text on my lock screen. Maeve. What does she want so urgently?

My head whips up. The car in front of me has slammed on its brakes. I do the same and barely stop in time. If my tires screech, I don't hear them.

Then the tug of my seat belt relaxes, and I fall back into my seat, feeling the rapid rise and fall of my chest. Brake lights are blinking on and off everywhere I look. A cloud of smoke or dust rises ahead along the road. An accident!

I crane my neck to see better, but the car in front is a ridiculously huge 4WD that takes up the entire lane. The driver looks tiny inside it. She's not getting out, so I assume there's no need for me to do so either. Anyway, what use would a deaf guy be in a crisis, even if I did know first aid? I could ask questions but not hear the answers.

The right lane starts moving again. Indicators flash. Gradually the stalled traffic merges and flows around the scene, which turns out to be a rear-end collision between a red pickup and a taxi in the leftmost lane. Steam pours from a busted radiator.

The drivers stand on the side of the road, exchanging details. No road rage in evidence. I keep my eyes peeled for flashing lights, just in case the police have been called and I need to get out of the way.

Then I'm past and accelerating, leaving behind everything, apart from a shaky feeling in my entire body. If I hadn't noticed in time, that might've been me back there too, trying to explain to the driver of the big 4WD why I went headlong up her arse.

The sequence of events plays on repeat through my mind. Maeve's texts. Me looking down to read her name, then looking back up again to see red lights flaring. Slamming on the brakes—

Maeve's texts. Me looking down, then looking back up again to see red lights flaring—

Maeve's texts. Me looking down, then looking back up—

Me looking down, then looking back up—

—then looking back up—

My mental recall sticks here. There's something missing.

What made me look up?

I couldn't have seen anything to indicate that there had been a sudden impact in my vicinity. The phone had my full attention. I couldn't have felt anything, either. Not from inside the car. And I definitely couldn't have heard anything . . .

Could I?

My hands are shaking with more than just adrenaline. Almost sick with something that might be hope, except there's no word I know of for a feeling this desperate, I pull over and search my memory.

I have no recollection of hearing anything, and surely I *would* remember that. But what if it's not that simple? What if the hearing part or parts of my brain are only slowly growing back?

I try clicking my fingers and clapping my hands. I turn on the radio as high as it'll go. Maeve has it set to some shitty commercial station, but I don't care. Straining, I hear . . . I hear . . .

Nothing.

I sag, unsure whether to feel hope or despair. Maybe my memory has the timing all mixed up—after all, it happened in an instant.

I think of G and everything she's going through. I warn myself not to get too excited about something that might never happen.

G is waiting for me. My hands are steadier now, so I put the car in gear.

Remembering the texts from Maeve, I read them before pulling back out into the traffic.

What's her name?

When do I get to meet her?

Come on, big brother, YOU OWE ME.

"PEYOTE SQUEAL"

November 6

Maeve was born thinking I owed her, but sometimes she's right, and not just for pushing me out of the car the night I argued with Mum.

I fully expected no one to listen to "Pain Grade," so it was a surprise when people started leaving comments.

There was some criticism: *bending flat, copying Metallica, don't quit your day job, bullshit you're deaf* kind of thing. Someone complained that they could hear me humming along, which is flat-out impossible since I recorded straight from the effects pedals into my laptop with no microphone—unless the groaning ghost has supernatural powers.

Others were more complimentary, noting my chops, expressing amazement that I couldn't hear a thing (usually with lots of exclamation marks), and asking for more.

When Maeve left a comment, I knew why the recording was getting hits. She's way more active on social media than I am. Seeing my Deafman post and figuring out it was me, all she said was *He lives!* but the message was clear and appreciated. I'd been feeling dead for a while. I was warmed that she'd noticed my brief revival and felt moved to share.

That prompted the question, though: what was I going to do next?

Mia and Shari had left me feeling lonely and isolated, but recording and releasing "Pain Grade" into the wild definitely made me feel better. Perhaps, I reasoned, I should do more.

The second solo I released, "Shark Venus," was very different from the first. Cleaner sounds, experimental chords, long loops that folded back on themselves in strange, irregular ways. I have no idea if it sounded anything like what I was writing in the moment, in my head, but it gave me a feeling of completion and connection—and that's what I was looking for. Getting something out of my system and offloading it onto the internet.

Upload. Share. Wait. That's the mantra of the modern music mogul, right? Would-be mogul, anyway. I told myself I wasn't likely to become famous this way. I just wanted Deafman to be noticed by *someone*.

It was. The first comment on "Shark Venus" was a question from someone calling themselves GlanMaster.

Hey, are you starting a channel?

I hadn't responded to the comments on "Pain Grade," but I felt this deserved an answer.

Would you subscribe if I did?

Sure. I like a good laugh.

Don't feed the trolls, I reminded myself.

Mum, I told you not to comment here!

That earned me an LOL, which I suppose was something.

Setting up a channel was a double act of defiance, aimed at my circumstances as well as GlanMaster, who did subscribe and continued to listen and comment, if only to tell me how hilarious the whole exercise was. I wondered at first if he was a sock puppet for Roo or Sad Alan, but they couldn't have maintained such a pretense for so long. I know my friends as well as they know me. There's a limit to how hard they'll work for kicks.

"Peyote Squeal" followed "Shark Venus," and after that came "Crystal Tomato." The names meant nothing beyond a faint evocation of tone, but I'll confess I had fun with them. The Notes app on my phone is full of odd phrases I've copied from shop signs and graffiti, saved for possible band names. Some are misheard phrases or typos.

My family subscribed, although I suspect Mum never listened, and Maeve lost interest pretty much immediately. Dad was more involved. Occasionally he lifted a lick and made sure I was paid for it. He even had suggestions for how certain tracks could be improved. My general method was to explore an idea via improvisation until I felt it had the correct shape, then to pick a take that felt right to me. By "felt," I'm being literal: pressing my desktop monitors against my stomach, like Beethoven clenching a stick between his teeth and touching it to the piano while he played, I could feel the way the sound rose and fell. If I could've smelled or tasted the files, I would've done that too. Dad's feedback helped shape my instincts, giving me an idea of whether my gut was on the mark or not.

Each track took a couple of days spent pretty much nonstop playing and replaying. In the two months since my stroke, I'd been given a permanent pass from school and exams (a definite upside to losing my hearing) and had lost my part-time job, so time was one thing I had plenty of. My only obligations were deaf class and counseling, and I barely concentrated during them. When I started working on the files at Dad's place, mixing in effects, drum tracks, synths, and even vocals (the odd growl, where the urge took me), I knew it had become an overwhelming obsession. My subscriber list wasn't huge, but it was growing, and I felt I owed it to them to keep producing, if not to myself.

That's when a local reporter got wind of it and sent me an email. I think my old guitar teacher, Mr. Mackereth, had ratted me out. She said she wanted to do a story but that her paper would need something concrete to back it up.

Like a concert? A tour? Sad Alan's skepticism fairly dripped out of my phone's screen.

I won't feel comfortable playing live without you guys.

A video? I could film you. Add a filter. My sisters could dance, or whatever they call it, in the background. Roo was marginally more supportive, although as always I had a hard time telling if he was ripping on me or not. He had twin sisters, who had spoken their own language until they turned eight and now, at thirteen, still seemed like interlopers from an alien dimension.

Maybe I should cut a CD.

Yeah, I could give it to my gran for Xmas.

And put it up on the internet as well, I mean. Is that so dumb?

I dunno. How important is it to you? You know you'll probably only sell ten copies.

We'll buy one, won't we, Roo?

Yeah, anything for the Drip. But only one. You can keep it, Alan. I'll rip it.

They were right. It was a dumb idea. But it did matter to me, more than words could say. Maybe a CD could stand in for everything I couldn't hear.

What about a cassette? Dad's got an old duplicator somewhere.

Tapes are in again. That could work.

Alan, you reckon flares are coming back in. Are you serious, Drip?

Maybe. I could master it in the studio, knock together a cover I could print at home . . . You'd help put it all together, wouldn't you?

Miss the chance to make history? Never!

That was as big a vote of confidence I was going to get from those guys, so next I emailed Dad, who confirmed he still had the replicator, which produced six finished cassettes from a stereo master running at high speed. He also had some boxes of cassette blanks hoarded away in hope of the format's return.

Really takes me back, he said as he showed me how to work the ancient machine. The first album I ever owned was on cassette.

Back in the Stone Age?

The Rolling Stones Age, yeah. When I was a kid, you got one new album a week, if you were lucky.

Sounds brilliant.

Ah, well. It's all relative. You've absorbed ten times more music than I had by your age. I'll never catch up. Who has time to listen to anything new?

I'm pretty sure he was trying to make me feel better.

Me, I concentrated on having a physical object that I could hold up as evidence: *Look, there's hope!* Hope in the performance of music that people would hear and maybe even pay for.

I kept my newfound positivity clutched tightly to my chest, fearing that if I let go for an instant, it would be dashed.

STUCK IN LEAPS

December 30

New Year's Eve Eve brings me emotional déjà vu as I thread through sterile-smelling corridors, past nurses and patients and the occasional doctor, to find G sitting with her back against the bedhead, playing a game on her phone.

What's up? Why do you look weird?

Damn my body language for shouting when I want to be silent. I can't tell her about what happened in the car on the way here, because it wouldn't be fair. It might turn out to be nothing, anyway, like her "vagus nerve stimulation" treatment.

That's how I normally look. And I'm here to see you, not talk about me.

Nothing to see here. I'm being discharged today. Want to give me a lift home? Aunty Lou is at work. I'll give you her number if you want to check I'm not scamming you into breaking me out early.

No need. I trust you, god knows why.

I'm asking myself the same question. You forgot my coffee, didn't you?

I actually slap my forehead. Her vital beverage completely slipped my mind—understandably, I reckon, given what happened, but how can I explain the one fact without mentioning the other?

Sorry. Guess I'm more worried about you than you thought.

You should be worried about yourself. I've killed for less.

But she's smiling, so I sit down.

Want me to get some from the cafeteria?

She shudders theatrically.

I'd rather die.

The smile frays. We're thinking the same thing: *You almost did.*

I take her hand. She squeezes.

Tell me, I say. **If you want me to understand.**

G nods, and I hold the phone up to her lips. This is what it records:

I've talked to some of that tiny fragments of sounds songs speech background noises gets stuck in leaps over and over that it mean anything I've tried using hot to see if these and a siege and a but it's just nothing and lay out most of the time sometimes I can't sleep we didn't think when it fades out for beat until myself it's going finally the day comes back again always louder than into you have no idea

You know that once the enemy soldiers with no ways time she that heavy metals shit Eli 24 as a day that drives people crazy that really like this is driving me crazy like it squeezing me out of my own heat splitting the atom ideas And then per meal a affect sorry she said it was a long-shot new treatment isn't over yet but nothing's getting better it's never going to get data I tell myself I should stop lending sign language but that's like giving up and I never give up when of lewd is mad at me she stays on as stubborn and stupid as my mum table was that I don't know if she's just trying to shine me into being glued to your parents do that

I'm sorry I haven't told you any of these is never in the UK and he is someone is evident to me and I'm glad you're here and graduates a patient god knows what you're getting out of this just don't ever forget my coffee in all your data and

Watching the words trickle and stutter across the screen, most of them transcribed inaccurately but with occasional, powerful flashes of meaning, it really strikes me how frustrating, perhaps even pointless, this whole voice-recognition exercise can be. It's like that Google Translate game where you turn a sentence from English to Russian to Chinese to Spanish and then back to English, because the nonsense it produces is hilarious. Only this isn't making me laugh, and it isn't a game. It couldn't be more serious.

This is how we communicate, secondhand through apps. No wonder I've missed the full impact of what G's been going through.

She speaks for a long time, crying at one point. I lie down next to her on the hospital bed and watch as she edits the gibberish on the screen into sense.

I've told you some of it. Tiny fragments of sounds—songs, speech, background noises—get stuck in loops, over and over. They don't mean anything. I've tried listening hard to see if there's a message in there, but it's just . . . nothing. And loud, most of the time. Sometimes I can't sleep, or even think. When it fades out for a bit, I tell myself it's going, finally, but then it comes back again. Always. Louder than ever. You have no idea.

I have some idea. She's been sharing hints of this ever since we started hanging out. Which is not to say that she's wrong for telling me again. I guess it hasn't penetrated my silent world, the truth of her private cacophony.

I think of the day at uni when I mimed the sound of Blackmod and feel faintly ill. I was making imaginary noise to fill my emptiness while she was trying to erase imaginary noises that she had too many of.

You know they torture enemy soldiers with noise, don't you? That heavy metal shit you like, 24 hours a day. It drives people crazy. Literally. Like this is driving me crazy. Like it's squeezing me out of my own head, squirting me out my ears.

And then Prameela . . . Ah, fuck, sorry. She said it was a long shot, and the treatment isn't over yet, but nothing's getting better. It's never going to get better. And sign language feels like giving up. When Aunty Lou is mad at me, she says I'm as stubborn and stupid as my mum ever was, but I don't know if she's just trying to shame me into being good. Do your parents do that?

Briefly interrupting her editing, I confirm that this indeed is the case. They learn the technique in parent school.

I'm sorry I haven't told you any of this. There's no room for you in here, Simon. There's no room for me. But I'm glad you're here. I'm glad you're so patient. God knows what you're getting out of this. Just don't ever forget my coffee again, or you're a dead man.

I laugh, and she kisses me, taking me by surprise with the force of it, the need. Naturally, I respond. This is what I want. She fills me when she's with me. When there's space for me, when the noise allows me in.

The bed shakes under us. We break apart and look up. A smiling nurse has banged the end of the frame. This is how you attract the attention of someone who can't hear. This is how you ruin a teenager's day.

The nurse has an iPad, which she uses like a whiteboard. She writes, *Time to check out?*

G gives her two giant thumbs-up, and I, blushing furiously, get off the bed and out of the way.

As I wait in the hallway for G to dress and pack, I think more about G's world. Hers is full where mine is empty. If only I could take on some of her burden. That might make life easier for both of us. I would have *some* sound, and she would have less.

For the time being, I am able to put aside the possibility that my brain is learning to hear again. Later, I will email Selwyn Floyd. I won't tell G. I feel like I am holding a candle between my cupped hands. Speak too freely, and it might just blow out.

G appears with a backpack slung over her shoulder, wearing strikingly conventional sneakers, tights, and hoodie. No black. The trim is actually pink.

Catching my eye, she shrugs. *Aunty Lou,* she mouths. When I mime taking a photo, she puts on a *not if you want to live* face.

Sometimes Auslan is simplest, and I know she knows the sign for *Where to?*

She gives me directions, starting with walking down the hallway.

Her house is near the beach. I can smell the salt and dead fish. Seagulls wheel across the western sky. The threat of rain has kept beachgoers at home, so I have no problem finding a parking spot. The electric gate across G's driveway is shut.

She inclines her head. *Coming in?*

I mirror the gesture and with added eyebrows. *Sure?*

She nods, puts one arm through the strap of her backpack, and opens the door of the car. I follow her, but not too closely, as she reaches over the fence, pushes a button, and the gate slides soundlessly open.

A dog bounds through the gap and throws itself at G and

me in turn. It's one of those little yappy dogs I loved to hate, back in my hearing days. I assume it's been barking at us from the other side of the gate the whole time we were standing there.

G ignores the dog, apart from holding its collar while she closes the gate. Aunty Lou's pet, then. Not something I'm obliged to make friends with.

She waves *Come on* and leads me up the path to a deep veranda. The home is an old austerity place built for soldiers after the Second World War, the kind Mum's always wanted to buy, but it's been touched up at least twice since, with mixed results. The original sandstone has been regrouted, and there's evidence of a second floor extruding through a red-tiled roof. The door is modern, and so is the security system. G keys in a number to spare the neighbors. A siren wouldn't remotely bother us, until the SWAT team arrives.

The dog stays outside. Inside is dark and warm. The air smells faintly of lemon, of her. Something reminds me of home, but it's not the furniture, which looks like it hasn't been updated for twenty years, or the books, which are everywhere. Aunty Lou loves a good romance novel, it seems. And why not? At least she reads. The last time Mum picked up anything romantic was when she was dating Dad—"And look how that turned out," she loves to say.

As I follow G past a kitchen bar with cane stools, thinking, *So this is where she eats,* it hits me: there are no plants, vases, statues, or the like to block the view of anyone who lives here. That's why this place reminds me of home. Someone has gone to a lot of trouble to preserve a direct line of sight for those who can't hear.

Again, Aunty Lou's work. Mum did the same. I wonder if they were given identical pamphlets by their GPs: *Surviving Your Child's Sudden Deafness . . .*

My gaze swings around to G. She's studying me studying her house, and I wonder if she's imagined me being here as often as I have. I feel suddenly self-conscious, and my heart does that little flutter again.

Dropping her bag on one of the stools, she mimes, *Drink?*

I shake my head.

Then she's kissing me again, and I stop thinking in words.

DEAFMAN

December 1

Mixing and mastering the *Deafman* cassette made me happier than I had been since the stroke. My only other project was "get used to being deaf," and it would be fair to say I had zero investment in that. I hadn't realized how bored and frustrated I had become. *Deafman* gave me a reason to get out of bed.

I stopped going to deaf classes completely. It wasn't as though I was being graded or anything; I just didn't bother turning up. I also stopped seeing my counselor. KO emailed Mum a couple of times, but she put him off, guessing that I was going through something that might lead me to a happier place.

The reporter and I had arranged to talk in two weeks. That was my deadline. I figured if I didn't have something concrete for her by then, I probably never would.

Dad helped implement this plan, but he let me make all the creative decisions. The cover had to be cheap, so I used a free photo of Blind Lemon Jefferson, touched up with eighties fluorescent highlights. On the flipside, by hand, I wrote the titles:

DEAFMAN

Side One:

1. "Triple Nine Great Integrity"
2. "Glam Gong"
3. "Blood Meal, Mouth Feel"
4. "Shark Venus"
5. "Peyote Squeal"

Side Two:

1. "Pain Grade"
2. "Transparent Art Gallery"
3. "Crystal Tomato"
4. "Sister of a Clown"

I played the master over and over against my stomach, against my thighs, even against my skull. I sat in Subaqueous Studios and watched the levels rise and fall so long they still danced when my eyes closed. I dreamed the album in all its colors and vibrations, the spooling tape, Blind Lemon's heavy-lidded sockets.

But I never heard it, not in my dreams or in real life. I never hear my dreams at all anymore, which I'm informed by the internet is weird. The part of my brain that died took that ability too.

When I could justify delaying no longer, I started duplicating. Roo and Sad Alan cut and folded the covers. Dad prepared labels to go on the cassettes. The four of us stuck them on over pizza, me watching their lips and my app as they talked about musicians Dad had played with through the years.

All this effort condensed down to just two boxes of finished product, plus an upload to the usual music streaming services. I put a copy in an express envelope to send to the reporter the next morning. We packed up our rubbish. My friends went home, and Dad went to bed.

I stayed in the cave all night long, staring at the steadily glowing lights and feeling like I'd forgotten something important.

The reporter, Madeleine Winter, who sounded like someone from *Game of Thrones,* messaged me a week later, which was perfect timing. The open box in my bedroom had emptied by about a third, with sales limited almost entirely to friends, subscribers, and family. Now that that audience was exhausted, I was thinking of doing something on social media to give it more of a nudge. Releasing bonus tracks for particularly generous supporters, say, or taking something very much like requests, although I had no intention of playing "Danke Schoen" or (worse) "Damage, Inc." so GlanMaster could have a giggle.

With Madeleine Winter in the loop, maybe the newspaper could do that for me. If I got really lucky, maybe I'd make enough to think about doing this for a living, and uni would be irrelevant.

We arranged a time to meet in a café the next day, one day short of my three-month anniversary. She asked, Will we need an interpreter?

We'll be fine, I messaged back.

Great. I have pink glasses, and I'll sit facing the door so you'll see me.

And if I get there first, I'm the one who looks like a heavy metal guitarist.

Of course! Haha.

Madeleine arrived ten minutes late, just as I downed the coffee I had negotiated with my waiter by writing on a napkin. She spotted me immediately—I was wearing a Dio T-shirt and kept my hair down so there could be no uncertainty as to my identity. She breezed over and settled opposite me with an apologetic expression.

"No worries, hi, nice to meet you," I said, causing her to practically jump back out of her seat.

OMG, she messaged me while I trained an app to recognize her voice. You can talk!

"Sure," I said. "I only lost my hearing recently."

I'm so sorry, my phone spelt out.

"What for? It's not your fault."

I mean . . . It's amazing. You don't look deaf at all.

I opened my mouth to ask her how I was supposed to look but thought better of it.

"This is working now," I said, putting the phone between us. She did the same with hers, to record the conversation.

That's pretty cool, she said about my app. Wouldn't it be easier to just read my lips, though?

"I can't do that, and anyway, it's not reliable."

What a shame. It'd be so great at parties. I've always wanted to learn sign language so I could talk to my friends without anyone else knowing what I was saying. I bet you do that all the time.

"Not really."

No, I guess it wouldn't work when everyone's deaf. Of course!

Madeleine laughed, and I noticed people glancing at her. She was talking too loudly.

"My friends aren't deaf," I started to explain, but again stopped myself. That wasn't what I was there to talk about. "So, the cassette . . . ?"

Oh yes, I listened to your album. It's intense. And no wonder. I love music. I'd kill myself if I couldn't—sorry, but you know what I mean? It'd be like breaking up with someone or losing a pet. It must rip your heart right out through your chest. Is that what you're trying to capture in these recordings?

"I was just trying to play guitar."

I know, right? And you play it so well! Are you sure you can't hear? At all? You haven't got one of those implant things you're not telling me about?

She laughed again, and I hope I didn't look as irritated as I was beginning to feel.

This was everything Sandra Mack had warned me about in our very first session. People won't understand, she had told me. Most have never met someone from the Deaf community, but that won't stop them having preconceived ideas, and it certainly doesn't stop them saying the same things everyone says. "Sign language looks so beautiful. Can you show me how to swear?" Maybe you've said things like this yourself—it's okay, no one's to blame. But now you'll be on the other side of the conversation, and there will be days it'll drive you mad.

I get that already because of my hair and my tatts, I had typed back with a shrug.

Sandra had said, You can cut your hair and have your tatts removed. This, I'm afraid, you'll have forever.

Then, as during this interview, my face had felt as if it was made of wood.

"Can't hear a thing," I told Madeleine Winter, "and never will. Because I had a stroke, three months ago, getting a cochlear implant isn't an option. The part of me that hears sound is gone for good."

So you have brain damage as well? My god, this story just keeps getting—I mean . . . Simon, you've overcome so much to make this album, this cassette. It really is incredible. And you did it all on your own?

"My father helped, and my friends."

They're so good to you. They must be very proud. How does that make you feel?

"Feel?" *Like shit,* I wanted to say. *And right now, like I'm being patronized and belittled.* I told myself to think of the sales. If the article went viral, it would totally be worth it.

"I feel like nothing's preventing me from being the artist I always wanted to be," I told her. "Not hearing doesn't stop me loving music, or experiencing music, or thinking about music. Music is all around us. It's in everything we do. Life *is* music, so until I'm dead, I'll keep making it."

Fine words, plus something of a challenge to both myself and the universe. She nodded enthusiastically, and I wondered if anything I was saying was getting through the way I meant it to.

Eventually her nodding slowed, and she told me she had enough for a story. A photographer would text later that day. Was there anywhere I could think of for a suitable shot?

I suggested Dad's studio, and she cheerfully agreed. Bring a guitar, she said. That T-shirt will be perfect. And make sure you buy the Saturday paper.

We stood and shook hands. She hurried off, late for her next meeting and leaving me feeling as though she'd taken all the breathable air with her.

Maybe the cassette would sell. But what else would change?

A coffee appeared in front of me. *On the house,* said the note on the napkin, accompanied by a surprisingly accurate caricature of Madeleine with drag queen makeup and horns. The waiter gave me a sympathetic smile and went back to the counter.

ADD THE D

December 31

I try not to resent Selwyn Floyd for being on holiday between Christmas and New Year, right when I need to see him. Luckily, Prameela Verma manages to fit me in. I sit nervously in her waiting room, considering my fingernails and reminding myself that I'm not making anything up.

It happened. I heard something.

Didn't I?

Any other day, my entire being would be focused on G and what occurred between us in the last twenty-four hours, from me taking her home to now. That *definitely* happened. When I breathe in, I smell her, even though I haven't seen her since this morning. I can feel her, taste her, too. Part of me is still in her room, in our soundless bubble where everything is *right,* even as the rest of me is freaking out.

It's dark in her room, just like I imagined it. No neater than mine, but cluttered in different ways. Clothes convene in her corners like I collect cables. Her books are ordered vertically as well as horizontally, like my CDs. Her posters are of dark fantasy series, where mine are of metal bands —and funnily enough, the makeup, scowls, and fonts aren't dissimilar. Her bed isn't made, but her sheets are clean, the antithesis of my bed. My feet dangled over the end. Mum rigged a new switch outside my door so she can flash the lights when she wants to come in; Aunty Lou installed a bolt on the inside.

I saw naked-wood scars on the door frame where the lock used to be.

There was no other evidence of what happened when G tried to kill herself, and I didn't ask about it. Maybe me coming over was a means of avoiding that subject, but it wasn't as though we didn't talk at all. We stayed up late typing into our phones so Aunty Lou wouldn't be disturbed by our too-loud voices. She knew I was there, just as Mum knew I wasn't coming home. We were considerate, discreet, and careful.

Leaving this morning was the hardest thing I've ever done.

I really have to go. I'm sorry.

I had booked the appointment with Prameela via email as soon as the clinic opened. G didn't know that I had done that; she was still asleep at the time, probably snoring, for all I could tell. When she woke, I told her this was something I'd locked in ages ago and couldn't get out of.

Do you want me to come back afterwards?

It's okay. Don't worry about it.

She seemed different this morning. Distant, distracted. I wondered if she regretted what had happened. I wondered what was going on inside her head. Then I saw her fingers tapping restlessly against her breastbone, one rapid rhythm, repeated over and over.

Is it loud today?

Instead of replying with words, she leaned into me and put her head against my shoulder. I took that as a yes. My fingers itched to say more, but I didn't. Anything I said would make things worse.

Thank you, she texted while I was en route to the clinic. Three more texts quickly followed.

I'll message you when I can, Simon.

Don't worry.

I'm not going anywhere.

And here I am, turning the phone over and over in my hand. *Give her space, give her silence*: that has to be my mantra. The last thing I want to do is drive her away.

A hand touches my left upper arm. Prameela leans into view, and I have to think for a moment to remember why I'm here. Seems my entire being did forget, after all.

Hi, she signs. *Come on through.*

I wave, a gesture, and follow her into her office.

Prameela's space is friendlier than Selwyn Floyd's sterile cavern. The chairs are made of a brown leather that gives comfortably underneath my weight. Her shelves are full of glass knick-knacks, handicrafts, and photos of small children. They don't look like her kids. Patients, perhaps.

You really should learn how to sign, Simon. It would make your life so much easier.

"*Your* life," I say, unrepentant for making Prameela speak via her iPad.

I get it. You're deaf, but you don't feel Deaf yet. That makes sense to me. The difference is not just whether you can hear or not. It's where you belong culturally. Until you can bring yourself to add the D to deaf, you're not part of the Deaf community: you're a hearing person who can't hear—but how long can that stance last? That defiance of the facts? You're going to need Auslan one day. If you learn it now, it'll be there for you.

Who made her my counselor?

"Yesterday," I tell her, "I think I heard something."

Prameela leans forward and erases her words from the screen with one deft swipe of her hand.

Go on.

She listens to my account of that moment in traffic once through, paying close attention, then asks me to tell her again, this time with questions. I am interrogated from all angles, including some I never thought of. Could I have seen a driver alongside me reacting out of the corner of my eye? Could cars have been slowing already before I glanced at the phone? Have I experienced headaches lately, or dizzy spells, or double vision? Have I been unduly stressed? How does the thought that I might be wrong about hearing again make me feel?

"Feel? No worse than usual."

Are you sure?

"Don't worry. I'm not like G. I mean George." Then I remember that Prameela probably doesn't know about the connection between us. "Another one of your patients. A girl. I met her in deaf class. You know, tinnitus? The whole, uh, vagus nerve stimulation thing?"

She nods. The connection is made, but she divulges nothing.

I don't want you to invest too much in this, Simon, she tells me. It's probably just one of those weird coincidences that happens sometimes, but if you like, I'll talk to a colleague. I can do that right now. Would you mind waiting for a few minutes?

"No, sure, okay."

She gets up and walks past me and out the door. I sit and wait as patiently as I can. Who is her colleague? What do they know about me? There have only been thirteen cases of cortical deafness in the history of medicine. Prameela knows as much as anyone.

No worse than usual. It would be fair to say that what I told her was a lie. The very thought that my hearing might be coming back has sent me into an emotional spin. Did it happen, or am I going crazy? Am I going crazy, or did it happen? I'm wearing a rut back and forth between those two thoughts, deeper and deeper.

My head whips around. Prameela is standing behind me, her hand on the handle of the door, which is closed. She is looking at me, studying me, with a clinical intensity that feels like a blow.

What just happened?

"Are you okay?" I ask her.

She crosses to the desk and picks up the iPad.

Did you hear that?

"Hear what?"

You didn't hear anything?

"No. Was I supposed to?"

But you turned around.

"I . . . don't know why. Something happened. I turned to see. What did you do?"

I slammed the door.

We stare at each other. I definitely didn't hear anything, but I definitely did turn.

Perhaps you felt the air move. Unconsciously.

"You were standing between me and the door."

Vibrations through the floor, then? Or perhaps you saw me moving in a reflection.

"Off what?" There are no mirrors, and her framed diplomas are too high to cast an image at the right angle.

Perhaps you did hear something, then.

"So why don't I remember it?"

That's the question.

Her eyes are alight with speculations too complex for me to guess at.

I want you to note when anything like this happens again, she writes on the iPad. In the meantime, let's do some tests. My receptionist will email you the details.

I think of the MRI, and my heart sinks a little. *Totally worth it,* I tell myself, *if it proves I'm going to get better.*

But will it? I feel oddly deflated, as though the ambiguity is itself a negative.

Remember, Simon: don't get your hopes up.

She has read me completely wrong. "Okay, I won't."

Seriously. Go home, think about something else. Say hi to George and tell her I'll see her soon.

Her smile is too knowing. But there is caring there, too, and I am hit with the understanding that Prameela's days must be full of people like me, who clutch at the slightest threads of hope as if they're lines to the lives they have lost. How many times has she seen those threads snap? Will mine be one of them? Like G's?

"Thanks," I tell her as I get up and leave the warm sanctuary of her office. I came seeking answers and am leaving with more questions than ever, but none of that is her fault. All I can do is follow her advice to the very best of my limited abilities.

"LIVE OR DIE"

December 31

In the parking lot, I text G. She hasn't replied by the time I get home, so I figure it's a safe bet I won't hear from her for a while. The harsh light of this summer day bears down on the oasis that enclosed us the last twenty-four hours. Reality is unremitting.

The first thing that catches my eye in the kitchen is not something to graze on, but Madeleine Winter's article, which Mum insists on keeping pinned to the fridge with the irrational number magnets I gave her for Christmas last year. It's been out almost a month now, and the sight of the clipping still makes me cringe.

Brave Headbanger's Battle with Brain Injury

Under that headline, the photo captures me in mid-riff with long hair spraying up and out like a halo. It looks ridiculous. Maeve has helpfully added a hook nose and pointy chin.

My friends are texting about New Year's Eve parties I can't muster the energy to go to. Tired, dispirited, and alone, I brace myself for a long night.

• • •

To: Grace Dorn

From: Simon Rain

Date: December 31

Subject: Impossible Music #2

Dear Professor D,

I know, I know, you need my submission next month. I'm going as fast as I can.

"Live or Die"

Once upon a time, in the 1980s, there was an Australian synthesizer called the Fairlight CMI. Way ahead of its time—you could take a light pen and draw a waveform across the screen, and it would play the sound that you had created. This work is performed entirely on a Fairlight that belongs to my father.

On the big screen at the back of the stage is an image of the last page of Mahler's Tenth Symphony laid flat, with the notes, staves, and other markings standing out, as though drawn with very thick ink. A red line moves diagonally across the page, taking on bumps and kinks as it goes.

That red line is fed into the Fairlight as a waveform, creating one long, continuously changing note—a note that is far too low for the human ear, but played so loudly the audience feels the room rumble around them like the ceiling's about to fall in. Their eyeballs literally shake in their sockets.

The last details that go into the computer are the stems

on Mahler's f's where he wrote "für dich leben! für dich sterben!"
There, the work comes to an end, like everything must, even if it never really existed in the first place.
Simon

To: Simon Rain
From: Grace Dorn
Date: January 2
Subject: Re: Impossible Music #2
Simon—
This is promising, although I think you need to work on the titles. Let the performance do the talking. For the next one, try being a minimalist.
Also, are you okay?

PART FIVE

I.T. CONQUERED THE WORLD

December 15

Madeleine Winter's newspaper article was an embarrassing disaster from the headline (who wants to be described as "brave"?) to the last line. Everything I told her went through the saccharine filter of her mind and emerged so syrupy and sweet I barely recognized myself or my life. I guess she found out about Dad because of the photo shoot at Subaqueous Studios, but I wish she hadn't. Under her pen I became a child prodigy following in his famous father's footsteps, untimely toppled from the pantheon of great guitarists by fickle fate, stubbornly striving on in defiance of adversity, etc., etc., gag gag gag.

At least she mentioned the cassette. I sold a few extra copies as a result, not viral quantities, but enough to recoup the costs. That only made me feel worse, though. What were my buyers expecting? I wasn't Jimi Hendrix. All I had to offer was nine tracks I would never hear . . . a poignant detail Madeleine exploited in the final paragraph, to my endless mortification.

Twelve days after my first date with G, I threw the remaining cassettes in our garbage bin.

Mum found them and brought them back inside. Reluctantly, I think, but determined to use them to illustrate her point. Failed attempts to restart music career? Counting Blackmod, two.

We need to talk.

That was the prewritten note she handed me from her perch on the end of my bed. I was sitting in a corner of my room, feet hard against an amp that hadn't been turned on for weeks, head slowly thudding against the wall.

"What about?"

Another ready note: *Your future.*

"Do I have one?"

Exasperation is easy to read, at least on Mum's face. Note three said, *I spoke to a course advisor at uni. They offer Auslan translators and transcripts for Deaf students. When you decide what courses you want to put on your new uni application, instead of music—*

I read no further than that.

"What do you mean, 'instead of music'?"

Mum looked confused for a moment. Whatever was on note four, it didn't match the response I'd given her.

Can—be—H-O-B-B-Y—

"No. And I'm not changing my application."

She signed *But—*

That was as far as I let her go. "Music is all I know. It's not a *hobby*. So what if I can't hear? I'll do more theory, more musicology to make up for losing performance . . . Maybe I'll take composition instead."

Mum thrust another note at me, in desperation, it seemed to me.

I.T. is a good career path. Or design. You won't have any trouble getting in, thanks to your midyear results, and you can work from home, communicate via email—

"I'm not interested in I.T. or design. Or sculpture or . . . astronomy or whatever you're going to suggest next. I've applied for music, and that's where I'm going to stay. If they'll have me."

How—you—know—they—will?

To indicate "they," Mum pointed in the general direction of the university.

For the first time, I thought hard about how this might actually work.

"Professor Dorn—I met her at winter school—she runs the advanced composition program. It's super hard to get into, but she's interested in all sorts of weird shit, and we're tight."

T-I-G-H-T—what?

"We've exchanged emails."

So she can get you into the program?

"I guess so, if she thinks I'm up to it. I'll ask her."

When?

"When I email her next!"

Then—we—talk?

"Yes, but not about I.T. I'm not doing I.T. Ever."

The more we argued, the more obstinate I became. Partly out of fear, because what if she was right to be worried? There was no chance of me getting into performance now that I couldn't hear; the obstacles were just too great. Neither theory nor musicology offered anything like the thrill of creating or performing. Composition was my only remaining hope of taking music further—but what if Professor Dorn *wouldn't* accept me into the program? Music is my passion. I love it so much I recorded a cassette I'll never hear, for Christ's sake. That seemed crazy to Mum, but it didn't to me. Just because she'd caught me throwing out the cassettes didn't mean I'd given up entirely. My brief dream of being a mogul was dead, but this dream would do instead.

Mum was talking and signing at the same time, but I had gotten lost somewhere in the finger-spelling, and then Maeve was in the room, and she was shouting at Mum. Not wanting to miss this latest development, I thumbed on my phone and tried to decipher the garbled text trickling across its screen.

One fragment stood out:

He knows what he wants to do, Mum. Why don't you just leave him alone and let him do it?

Maeve defending me? I couldn't believe it. Neither could Mum, obviously. She threw up her hands and stormed out of the room, making the floorboards shake as she went.

"Thanks, Maeve," I said.

It wasn't for you. When you're doing your music thing, you're at least tolerable.

She left me alone to chew over this abruptly clarified understanding of myself—not Maeve's parting shot, but what my determination to study composition might actually mean. "The Future" was something I'd never articulated in detail. Before losing my hearing, it had simply been assumed that I'd go to uni to do performance, with a career in music to follow. Maybe I'd be a huge star; most likely I would play like Mr. Mackereth did and tutor music students on the side.

The future was now even harder to map out.

I texted Mr. Mackereth that night, seeking his guidance and, hopefully, approval.

It's a tough life, he replied. I won't lie about that. It's hard enough even if you can hear. You should only do this if you're absolutely sure.

Mum wants me to do I.T.

Well, maybe you should consider that.

I couldn't. I'd rather die.

Well, then. I think you've answered your own question. Give it your best shot and see what comes of it.

The thing is, I looked up the course requirements for composition, and they're really tough. I need to submit a portfolio in order to get in. Do you think Deafman would count?

I don't know, Simon. You'd have to ask.

I knew he was going to say that. That was the obvious thing to do. I'd been putting off that task, however, afraid the answer would be no, meaning the effective end of all my dreams, the erasure of a future that I still wanted, despite everything, to be very much like the old one, but with performance swapped out for composition. Was that too much to ask for?

Mr. Mackereth had more to say.

The smartest teacher I ever had once tried to talk me out of a music career. It was the best advice I ever ignored.

But you did ignore it. And now look at you!

There's not much to look at, Simon. Apart from music, what have I got?

Apart from music, what matters?

If you really feel this way, nothing anyone says is going to make a difference.

I wish I could convince Mum of that.

She's just worried about you. And rightly so. She's afraid you're making life harder for yourself by choosing this path. If you want to bring her around, you'll have to convince her that's not the case.

How?

Don't ask me! I'm still trying to convince my mother . . .

Mr. Mackereth signed off to put his eighteen-month-old son to bed—*thankfully, a child whose musical displays involve nothing more ambitious than banging two pots together*—and I lay back on my own bed to consider his words. On the one hand, he was spot-on: Dad had made it very clear to me that no one made money from the arts unless they were extraordinarily lucky. One day the royalties to "Tokyo Go" would dry up and he'd be as poor as the next musician.

On the other hand, what was money, really? Wouldn't it be better to be poor and doing something I loved than rich and doing something I hated?

Not that getting rich at anything was a guarantee. Knowing my luck, I'd be poor *and* stuck in a job I hated. I swore to do everything in my power to avoid that eventuality.

A LITTLE FRANKINCENSE

December 17

After our confrontation, Mum forced me to go back to KO. I had no good argument to avoid our sessions, since *Deafman* was done and Roo and Sad Alan were too busy playing in Slave Leia to practice with me. The only other person I had willingly spent any time with lately was G, and as enjoyable as I had found roller derby and our brief make-out session, it didn't seem fair to co-opt her as a convenient excuse.

Time had neither altered KO nor lessened his interest in my case. He had seen the article and wanted to know how it made me feel, so I gave him one of the cassettes Mum had rescued from the recycling bin and told him to listen to it. Explain in words, was the response he typed into our shared document.

Like I'm shouting into a pillow, I told him. **Smothered.**

By the reporter's inability to understand? I thought the interview was an exercise in selling more copies of the cassette.

I had to admit that it started that way.

But she didn't want to talk about the music. Not really. All she wanted to talk about was me losing my hearing.

You DID lose your hearing, though.

KO finger-spelled *D-E,* and I thought he was going for *deaf,* but with a grin he finished *R-P.*

I know, I know. But I want to be more than deaf.

How?

Like . . . I want to be a musician, not a DEAF musician. Being deaf shouldn't be who I am just because I can't hear.

Does it help to tell you that this is what it's like to be in a minority?

Not really, but—

You were born a healthy white male, Simon. You've grown up in a bubble of privilege. Now the bubble has popped, and you're living in the world most people inhabit. People of color, for instance, or genderqueer, adoptees . . .

I get it. You sound like Mum.

Because we're both right. But I understand: it doesn't help, being told WHY you're hurting WHILE you're hurting. If dentists . . . no, that doesn't bear thinking about. He rubbed his jaw, obviously speaking from recent experience. All right. Here's what I think we should do. We're going to conduct a ritual.

A what?

Our modern world has forgotten the power of rituals to help us transition through difficult phases in life. The

rituals we DO have sometimes seem designed to embed
feelings of emotions like fear, anger, and grief rather
than help us deal with them. For instance, the way you
spend so much time at your father's studio. That's a
ritual, of a kind. What does it do except reinforce the fact
that you can't hear? I want us to try something different,
something that might shock you out of the state of mind
you're in, into one that's more accepting of possibilities.

If it involves sacrificing chickens, count me out.

Nothing as metal as that, I swear!

KO made a sign I remembered from deaf class because it was the same as one from childhood: a cross drawn across the heart: *Promise*.

Let's see . . . I can fit you in tomorrow at five. Go home
and make a collection of things that remind you of music,
things you're prepared to let go of. If they'll burn, all the
better.

What the hell?

Trust me, Simon. I've done this before. It can be very
powerful.

I gave in, figuring this wasn't an argument I could win. Besides, what did I have to lose?

Do I have to wear anything special?

Unfortunately, this isn't *Harry Potter*, either. Just come as
you are and keep an open mind.

With a kind of wary trepidation, I did as he said, perusing

my bedroom during the sleepless hours for anything that might be suitable. It was amazing how much I had accumulated since holding my first guitar. *That* wasn't going on my pile of potential burnables, but my first music lesson book did. Various scraps of paper I'd written progressions on that had become songs for bands I'd played in. A series of Post-it notes on which I had tried to turn T. S. Eliot's "The Hollow Men" into lyrics. The poster of infamous rock guitars that had hung over my bed for more years than I could remember. The sleeve of a T-shirt ripped in the mosh pit of my first Bring Me the Horizon concert. *Deafman*. A copy of Madeleine Winter's newspaper article, retrieved crumpled from the bin.

To that pile I added a random selection from the notes that Selwyn Floyd had written to me during our early consultations, and the brain scan on which my damaged area had been highlighted. If we were exorcising ghosts, as a quick Google search suggested this ritual might be aspiring to do, I'd be happy to get rid of those.

The next day, Mum came home early to drive me to the clinic. I didn't twig that she was going to be part of the ritual until she insisted on coming in with me. Dad was there too, and Sandra Mack. It was a regular reunion.

KO awaited us in his office. He had prepared big cards with messages written on them, like in Bob Dylan's "Subterranean Homesick Blues" video. The first simply said, *This way,* and we followed as he led us outside, into the parking lot behind the back of the building. There, we found a waist-high steel drum that had clearly done incinerator duty before. Its interior was scorched black and exuded a fragrant charcoal smell.

We are gathered here today, said KO's next card, displayed once everyone had finished saying hello. I rolled my eyes. Mum shot me a stern look.

to help Simon bury the past
that's standing in the way of his future
while here in the present
I'd appreciate it if you kept this a secret
or I'll totally be fired
(you may laugh at my joke now)

KO gave us a card each and made tearing motions with his hands. We did as he instructed, ripping the messages into strips and placing them on a mound of twigs and firelighters in the barrel. When that was done, KO handed me a box of matches.

I shrugged, lit one, and set the paper ablaze. The small gathering made room for me as I moved around the barrel, making sure the fire reached everywhere. It took three matches to get the flames really going, and by then my head was ringing from the scented smoke rising up from the smoldering twigs. It smelled nothing like cigarettes or dope. This was silkily smooth and full of fine, white ash.

KO gave me a thumbs-up, then indicated that I was to start throwing stuff onto the fire.

It was harder than I expected. With each item, I felt a small tug, deep down inside me, like I was tearing out part of myself and tossing it into a grave. This wasn't just any old ritual, I perceived: it was a full-on funeral for the things I loved and, most tragically, for the part of my brain that had made me who I was.

My eyes watered, which might have been the smoke, but seeing me wipe tears away, Mum came and gave me a hug. Then the wind turned, and smoke enveloped us. We broke apart, coughing.

The last thing to go on the fire was the cassette of *Deafman*. It bubbled and blackened along with all the hopes and dreams I had entertained.

Except they didn't. They were still there, burning a giant hole in my heart. Meanwhile, nothing new rushed in to take their place.

Sandra Mack took Dad's hand and reached for mine. That did it. No way was I forming a happy-clappy circle over the cremation of my dreams.

"I'm going inside," I said. "This smoke is giving me a headache."

I waited in KO's office for the others to join me. He came in first, holding a fire extinguisher in one hand. Tugging open the bottom drawer of his desk, he placed it inside. For next time, I guessed.

Mum, Dad, and Sandra came next. There weren't enough seats, so Sandra stood by the door. KO produced a second laptop and invited them to type.

"This is bullshit," I said aloud instead, to forestall anything too upbeat. "Burning magic firewood in a parking lot isn't going to make anything better."

Sandra's hands moved, translating. I recognized the sign for "bullshit." But who was she signing for? Not me, surely, because I was the one who had spoken.

She was looking at KO, who nodded, and suddenly I felt very, very small.

KO was Deaf. I had never known. Either I hadn't noticed or I hadn't cared, and I wasn't sure which made me feel worse.

I told you it wouldn't be magic, KO typed on his own laptop, turning the screen so I could read. It WAS a special mix of firewood, though. Ivy, holly, birch, elder, pomegranate, wormwood, and a little frankincense for good measure—for transformation, renewal, rebirth, that kind of thing. My boyfriend is into this. He shrugged. I'm sorry it didn't help.

You tried, typed Mum. Thank you.

Yeah, thanks, I typed back, shamed into being more gracious by my faux pas. I felt as bad as Madeleine Winter: he didn't *look* deaf . . .

I know you're all just trying to help me do . . . this. Be Deaf. And maybe I can. In time. I guess I'll have to, or else life is going to be pretty fucking confusing.

Everyone made encouraging faces, and Sandra typed Yay you! on the laptop.

But I don't see why that means I have to give up everything, I went on. **The silence in my head doesn't mean music doesn't**

exist. Right? It's still out there. And still in here. I tapped my chest. I just need to find a way to bring it out so I can enjoy it too. I need . . .

There, words temporarily failed me. My innermost thoughts said, *I need everything to go back the way it was,* but the greater part of me was beginning to understand that that wasn't ever happening. Perhaps with a little more practice throwing out the things that were no longer relevant, I could find a way forward that didn't involve constantly torturing myself with what couldn't be . . .

I pictured myself standing over another bonfire, holding my black Schecter Omen in one hand and signing *Goodbye* with the other.

No, I told myself. *That isn't an option.*

I think I just need time. More time. To try studying composition at uni. If that doesn't work, then we can talk about something else.

All right, typed Mum. If Professor Dorn will let you in.

I'll email her today. I promise.

Deal.

Mum and I shook on it. Forced into a corner by life and KO, what other option did I have?

That wrapped up the wake. Sandra Mack signed goodbye and went to deal with her own clients. Dad patted KO on the shoulder and didn't go near Mum, which meant that he didn't come near me either, and that left me feeling a little wounded, considering we hadn't really communicated since the night in the studio. Did he think I was still angry at him? Or was he angry at me for making Mum angry at him? When he was gone, KO pressed a small cloth bundle into my hand, like one of those potpourri sachets Mum keeps trying to sneak into my dresser drawers. It smelled like the bonfire before we'd put it to the torch, and with good reason. It too contained a mixture of ivy, holly, birch, elder, pomegranate, wormwood, and a little frankincense for good measure.

Stephen made it, KO typed. I'll be in trouble if I don't give it to you. Let's humor him, shall we?

I signed, ***Thanks,*** and he signed the same back. I slipped the sachet into my backpack, wishing it really did have the power to solve all my problems.

There was a message from Dad waiting on my computer when I got home from Deaf Solutions.

Simon—

Well, that was a load of wank. But it made me think about your mother and me—no don't hit delete! I'm not going to talk about our sex life. Hold that thought for your 21st.

One of the reasons she and I broke up is because I'm terrible at committing to things. Just awful. It may not look that way because I've got the business and have been in bands, etc., but I'm only in them when they're safe, and once they stop being safe, I run. That's why I stopped playing for Contact, right at our peak. I'd rather be behind a mixing desk than in a spotlight, even with my mates.

I see a bit of me in you. Lots of your mother, luckily—but everything to do with music, and a bit of my fear of joining in. You definitely get those from me.

I think that's what the whole funeral thing today was for. The words KO wrote didn't matter. It was about bringing us together, so you'll know you're not alone, no matter how much you might want to be right now. Hiding behind the mixing console of your life isn't going to work. Just look at how things turned out for me.

Anyway, this is probably the longest message I've ever sent you. Here's some <trippy hippies> to make up for it.

Love, Dad.

I didn't respond. Although I felt better for knowing that he hadn't meant to brush me off and I'll admit that I might have teared up a little on reading his words, what did they solve? Nothing. His email was just another ritual designed to make someone else feel better, like he was helping when actually he wasn't. What "mixing console" was I supposedly hiding behind? The one in his studio, literally as well as metaphorically?

My promise to Mum weighed heavily on me until I actually made good on it. Perish the thought that the thing I shared with Dad was actually a fear of powerful women.

Fortunately, that was easily dismissed.

To my amazement, Professor Dorn replied within five minutes to my request to study composition.

A deaf composition student? Are you serious?

I don't know if you realize it, but once every year, all the music teachers in the country get together to brag about their students. The ones who've won awards, the ones who've had pieces performed, the ones who've got real jobs. But it's the ones who've struggled against the greatest adversity to get a passing grade that really make us shine. The brainless, the clumsy, the lazy. The bigger the challenge, the bigger the kudos.

I've been slipping down the tables lately, so keep talking!

(Everything in this email is a lie except for the last three words. Seriously, let's talk.)

When you've got little left to lose, any victory feels immense. I played some air guitar to celebrate.

Then her second email arrived:

Oh, I meant to say, improvisation is not composition, so whatever goes in your portfolio, it can't be Deafman. *Sorry. Try again. You've got until February.*

I groaned. There went that plan. But I wasn't ready to give up yet. I would just have to come up with something else. The alternative, resigning myself to facts and figures and a life without music—Mum and Maeve's vision of the perfect future, not mine—was too awful even to contemplate.

"SUBTITLE SONATA"

January 3

There's no such thing as unmusical sound. Fine. That's been my philosophy ever since I realized that noise music exists. But is there such a thing as musical un-sound? Proving that it might exist, or attempting to, is how I fill the first days of the new year, while waiting for G to get back in touch, for the second round of test appointments to finish, and for Professor Dorn to respond to my most recent ideas. Fear is a great motivator.

Impossible Music #3:
"0.00005"
Mechanically, the human ear is limited by its ability to perceive sounds above certain durations. In other words, if an event happens too quickly, we can't hear it at all. That's why notes higher than 20,000Hz are inaudible. Each prerecorded work in this series is performed so quickly that not only can individual notes not be discerned, but the entire work will pass unnoticed. This

doesn't limit the size of the works themselves: they could range from a short sonata to an entire symphony, played very, very fast. In the end, they'll all flash by in an instant.

At the exact moment when each work is broadcast into the performance space, the lights will switch on and then off again, generating a very bright, multicolored flash that will leave the audience feeling like they have just missed something. It's too late for them to hear it. It's gone, finished, over—forever.

The title of this series reflects that fact that one cycle at 20,000Hz lasts 0.00005 of a second. You can't get more minimal than that.

In answer to her earlier question, I told Professor Dorn that I would be okay when I got into the composition program. *Hint-hint.*

There's nothing I can do to make her response materialize any quicker, so in the meantime I conduct tests of my own devising to see if my maybe-hearing is getting any more reliable. For one, I slam doors like Prameela did and strain my damaged brain for the slightest sound. For another, I turn my phone's sound back on and tell Roo and Sad Alan to text at random times. Finally, I glitch a volume pedal and close my eyes while playing power chords through my dusty amp, never sure whether it's making any sound or not.

All this does is make Maeve annoyed.

LOUD NOISES I'LL GIVE YOU LOUD NOISES, she scrawls in all caps on the whiteboard. Then she opens her mouth and screams.

Did you hear that? I yelled "SHUT THE FUCK UP!"

I didn't hear a thing, but her lip movements and facial expression were pretty unambiguous.

"All right," I tell her in defeat. "Sorry."

You all right?

"I'm fine," but then I realize that she signed the question instead of writing it down. For a second, to the part of my brain that processes language, it didn't make a difference.

With a cry of frustration and rage, I pick up a handful of *Deafman* cassettes from a pile on my desk and throw them against the opposite wall. Maeve ducks. Pieces go everywhere. I don't hear the crash and clatter.

I collapse back onto the bed and put my hands over my face. This isn't fair! Maybe I can't hear. Maybe I can't get into uni. And now it's becoming natural to view the world through the filter of silence—but I don't want any of it. I want, I want, I want . . .

My phone buzzes, and I pull it out of my pocket, thinking it might be G answering my prayer.

It's Maeve.

You want to smash shit? Come with me.

I look up. She's in the doorway, studying me over the upper edge of her phone. I have no idea what she's talking about, but

I nod, glad I haven't scared her away. Which is surprising, after all the door slamming and theatrics.

She takes me into the spare room, which we've used as a hangout as long as I can remember. It contains some half-empty storage boxes, a raggedy couch, an old TV, and a selection of gaming platforms that all belong to Maeve.

I've never had much interest in gaming, except with Sad Alan and Roo. On losing my hearing, that kind of activity quickly grew tiresome. You can type and game at the same time, but playing with friends in the same room is mostly about talking shit to each other or egging each other on. I haven't looked at a game for over three months.

Maeve points at the couch, and I slump into it while she switches things on and fiddles with settings. It's amazing how much she reminds me of Mum sometimes. They share a blunt triangular nose and strong jawline that gives them a mountainous profile, particularly when determined to get their own way. Eyes green, hair brown. They differ in skin tones: I'm dark, like Mum, where Maeve has Dad's Scandinavian creaminess.

The screen comes to life. She hands me a controller and sits next to me.

The controller buzzes with haptic life as lurid colors explode onto the screen. The opening of a game called *Demolition of the Damned* starts to play. The action is captioned.

Some places are born bad. Others are made that way.

<ominous music>
"No, don't, please—"
<Satanic shrieking>
<sound of blood splashing>

Maeve skips past the intro with a *you don't need to know all that* wave. Then we're straight into a session that teaches me how to navigate on the run through a haunted asylum, smashing doors open with my shoulder or booted foot, snatching up rusted knives and bottles of tainted medicine, and throwing them with growing speed and skill. The weapon every player starts with is a crucifix balled up in a fist. It's a shield, too: drop it, and you're demon fodder.

My mission is to tear the cursed place to the ground.

Maeve and I play exorcists well versed in the art of annihilation, careening through the game leaving a swath of rubble behind us. I can't hear the destructive power of our holy fists, but I can feel it through the controller, and even a little through my body. Maeve must have the volume turned up high for her own benefit, if not mine. Animated splinters fly. Blood splatters, in all different colors. Bone crunches.

And it is brilliant, just what I need. I shrug off my everyday concerns and completely immerse myself in the ludicrous violence of a game that technically Maeve shouldn't be playing, since it's rated R. But who cares about that? An hour flies by, then another, and I hardly think about anything else.

I'm so grateful I could kiss her. Almost.

We take a break to make toasted cheese sandwiches.

Your laugh is really loud now, she writes on her board.

"Sorry."

No, it's an improvement.

My phone buzzes again, and this time it is G, inviting me to dinner. I feel as though all my fortunes have turned at once.

With Aunty Lou. Just the three of us, nothing spesh. She's a good cook, but she's a vegetarian, so there won't be any meat. Is that okay?

Yes. We're cool?

I'm sorry I opt out like that. I can't help it. When someone's screaming in your ears, it's hard to concentrate on anything else. I don't mean you.

I figured. What good would screaming at you do?

None at all. And you get that now, right?

I get that.

So, great. See you at seven?

It's a date!

Pathetic. X

I put the phone back in my pocket, and Maeve gifts me with a sandwich and a significant look.

"What?"

She does a little *you're in lo-ove* dance, and I roll my eyes. But secretly I am pleased. If it's that obvious, it must be real, right?

And if my sister is making me lunch and making me feel better, life can't be completely awful.

We don't dwell on it. An infinite number of psychotic psychologists await our righteous fists.

To: Grace Dorn

From: Simon Rain

Date: January 3

Subject: Impossible Music #4

I've decided to change the titles.

#1 "Concerto for the Other"

#2 "Pedal Point (for Gustav)"

#3 "Miniatures"

And now, in case these three haven't already convinced you of my brilliance:

"3 of 4" or "Subtitle Sonata"

This work is composed for a trio of projectors. It unfolds through three different representations of the music in three different colors: (1) progress through a score (written for four voices), (2) the unfolding of notes on a sequencer, and (3) a verbal description of the work for those who can't read music. The score becomes increasingly complex as it unfolds until it overwhelms the capacity of musical notation, step-programming, or English to capture it.

This replicates the experience of reading closed captions that are largely ineffective at conveying the dialogue, foley, and soundtracks of modern media. Which is the "true" depiction of the actual thing? Is it one of the three, or all of them? If the latter, how is it possible to keep track of three streams at once?

As the work unfolds, each projection takes up more and more space on the screen until they overlap completely, creating a jumble of notes, data, and words that are increasingly difficult to separate. Finally, the black negative space vanishes, leaving the questions: Where is there room for the audience to bring their own experience to the performance? Where is the music itself, if there is no audio component, just visual? When the representation overwhelms the senses, how is that different from random noise?

The sonata finishes with all three projectors on full. The three colors overlap to form white. We have returned to where we started, perhaps no wiser.

Repeat ad nauseam.

Sorry if this is a bit rushed. I've somewhere important to be. You'll tell me when I've done enough, won't you?

Rain

To: Simon Rain

From: Grace Dorn

Date: January 3

Subject: Autoreply: Impossible Music #4

I am recovering from surgery for carpal tunnel syndrome and therefore unable to reply to emails.

If you're a postgrad seeking an extension, you are likely the cause of this problem. Please find someone else to belabor with your excuses.
Most sincerely,
Professor Dorn

GLOWING SPEECH BUBBLES

January 4

Dinner that night is a welcome distraction from one problem I can't solve, but it's also a reminder of another. Aunty Lou doesn't allow mobile phones at the table, a rule we used to have at home until it became one of the main ways we communicate. At Aunty Lou's, our choices are notes on paper, signing, or sitting incommunicado.

The meal itself is fantastic. G doesn't eat all of it, so I help myself to her leftovers rather than see it go to the dog, Rusty, who fusses for scraps at Aunty Lou's ankles. Also, while I'm eating, my hands are acceptably occupied and therefore too busy for Auslan. G fills in the answers to a lot of Aunty Lou's questions, like: I'm a musician; no, nothing she'd like. Brave? Nah, thick as a brick, more like.

I'm secretly, if a little irritably, impressed with how well G can sign now. This not a skill she ever revealed in private.

You don't like to sign, Aunty Lou writes to me when I'm done with dinner. *Are you learning to lip-read instead?*

I shake my head. "Too hard," I tell her, which compresses

into two words very little about my feelings on sign language —not to mention centuries of bitter arguments about how best to teach the deaf to communicate. Signing (manualism) or lip reading (oralism)? My answer is currently, *Surely there's a third option!*

George only signs to avoid writing me endless notes, Aunty Lou tells me.

G snatches that particular note out of my hand and puts her right closed fist emphatically into her open left hand: *True.* Then she gets up to clear the plates. I go to help, but Aunty Lou pulls me back down.

She smiles innocently until G is out of the room. Then she produces a note from her sleeve—prewritten, just like Mum's were when she tried to get me to give up on music—and slips it across the table. It says:

> *George is happier than I've seen her for a long time. Thank you. We still need to look after her, though. She's very fragile. I've thrown out everything she could use if she tries again, but of course there are other ways, and she is very determined. You'll tell me if you suspect anything, won't you? I'm sorry if I'm being too pushy or putting you under pressure. This is all very new to you.*

Underneath she's written her mobile number. I turn over the note and write on the other side.

I'll text you later, so you'll have my number.

Maybe do it now. Then destroy this note to stop it falling into the wrong hands, if you know what I mean.

Her eyes twinkle at our little conspiracy. Behind the humor, though, is a deep well of worry and sadness. She knows G better than I do, and if she is concerned . . .

But I know G in a different way, and the fact that G is trying to make room for a relationship gives me hope that she won't need us tiptoeing around her, watching her every move.

While she is out of the room, I sneakily save Aunty Lou's number under a fake name in case G sees it ("Orianthi") and text her, Mission accomplished.

Then I eat the note, and Aunty Lou laughs.

I wake with a jolt. Someone is pulling my hair! It takes a second to remember where I am and who the culprit must be.

G is thrashing back and forth, holding her hands up in front of her face, and has become entangled. Tear trails gleam in the merest hint of light. She is having a nightmare.

Gently unknotting myself, I sit up and take her wrists, feeling their lumpy scars against my skin. Unthinkingly, I make a soothing noise deep in my throat, even though she won't be able to hear it.

"G, shhhhh, wake up, G, shhhhh."

Her eyes flicker open and the muscles in her arms relax, but she is confused, still weeping. I let her go, give her space if she wants it.

She wraps herself around my chest and holds on tight until whatever torment visited her in her sleep subsides.

For the second time that week, I have stayed the night, and we are both more and less comfortable with each other than before. Now there's familiarity as well as newness: layers are forming over our initial impressions, like sediments in a deep ocean. I know all about her second tattoo and other hidden intimacies I could once only imagine. The way her skin feels, her lips, her hair. How she moves, tastes, breathes. I have misremembered nothing, and it all still feels fresh. Precious. Fragile.

When she is calmer, we lie entwined and whisper into our phones. The screens are like glowing speech bubbles, held up in front of our mouths. Words appear as though drawn by an invisible hand.

You must think I'm fucking insane.

Well, you know what they say about the crazy ones.

That we're the best at everything?

You got it. What were you dreaming about?

My second fall. I thought I was going to die, even when I regained consciousness. It was worse when I woke up than the first time, because the noise was louder, and I didn't understand what was going on. I thought I was in hell.

Do you still feel that way?

Part of me does. Don't be disappointed, like Aunty Lou. I know everything could be much worse. It can always be worse, right?

Sure. You could've landed on a patch of leprosy, or woken up in the year three million, when everyone is descended from Donald Trump, or—

Stop! I've had enough nightmares.

We kiss for a while, our text bubbles empty. When we come up for air, I do my best to reassure her on one point.

I honestly don't think Aunty Lou is disappointed in you.

Why? Did she say something?

Not about that.

Did she tell you?

Tell me what?

That I stole her stash of green dream to, you know, do it?

I fight the instinct to tense up, even though I'm suddenly dangling over the conversational precipice of her suicide attempt. How we got here I don't rightly know, but we are here, and I can't ruin this opportunity to understand by prying too hard.

What's green dream? If you tell me Aunty Lou's doing something hard like heroin, I'm not going to believe you.

She's not. It's a sedative. She belongs to a club of oldies who hoard it for when they are ready to die. Nembutal, it's really called. Better than a plastic bag or a razor blade. I speak from experience.

The phone is misunderstanding more of her words than usual, so I know her tone is different. How, though, I can't tell. Tighter, probably. She feels that way against me.

You don't have to tell me.

I want to. I'm still working it all out myself. I swiped Aunty Lou's stash and got the dose wrong—but maybe I did that deliberately? Was I just trying to get attention?

Maybe you needed attention?

Maybe. May fucking be. God, I'm so tired of this. Don't you ever get tired of it, the inside of your own head? The endless round and round of it all? I bet you don't. You always seem so calm, so in control. Just tell me your secret, and I promise I'll be sane. Probably.

Me? In control? Wait until I show you the cassette I made.

The what?

Long story. I was afraid to show you because you'd laugh. Yes, I get tired of it. I feel like I'm going in circles inside the world's biggest, darkest cave, and no matter how much I try, I can never touch the sides. But I never stop feeling as though at the very next step I'm going to walk into a wall.

Ah. For me, the wall is always smacking me in the face, and nothing I do gets me away from it.

You know, sometimes I envy you.

That's the saddest thing I've ever heard. Not heard—you know.

So what keeps you going?

Except for when it isn't? Habit, I guess. What about you?

I shrug, feeling it's neither fair nor completely true to say, *You*. I still have the possibility of studying composition, and now the tantalizing hope that my brain might be healing. But if I'm brutally honest with myself, not completely true is still mostly true, who cares about fair when this might be the only chance you have to tell someone they matter? That they matter a lot.

You.

It took you a long time to say that.

I didn't want it to sound dumb.

How can one word sound dumb?

I don't know. "Whom" could probably do it.

Simon Rain, I think I like you very much.

Is that so?

Yes.

We don't talk much after that, not because there isn't still a lot to say, but because there aren't words. And our hands are busy elsewhere. Given the choice between absorbing every living moment with her and discussing why she tried to commit suicide, the former wins every time.

Eventually, we fall asleep, and when I wake up, she's already in the shower. There's a text from her on my phone:

Got a meeting with Prameela at ten. Want to come say hi?

My first, panicky concern is what will happen if G finds out I've been having tests behind her back—but then sanity returns. Prameela won't say anything to G about another client.

Besides, it's not as though my hearing is flooding back in one triumphant wave. Or maybe even at all.

My battery is almost flat because I left my voice recognition app running overnight. What it has transcribed is very odd.

Don't be disappointed.

Don't be disappointed.

Don't be disappointed.

. . .

Hard like heroin.

Hard like heroin.

Hard like heroin.

Hard like heroin.

. . .

You.

You.

You.

You.

You.

This is how I discover that G talks in her sleep.

THANKS THROAT CANCER

December 20

Deafman wasn't the only thing I'd kept from G for fear of her mockery. My second attempt at giving Professor Dorn a portfolio to prove I could write music was another.

Writing music isn't all that difficult. Writing *good* music is. You can start with all the rules, conventions, and templates that even the laziest composer can follow and come up with something that isn't wrong and isn't awful . . . but at the same time isn't brilliant, or maybe not even good in a way that matters. Determining what sits on what side of that line is the trickiest part of the process. Usually it involves listening.

That, however, was obviously not an option for me.

On learning that I had to come up with something more substantial than guitar solos, my first thought was to give up in frustration. How could my *Deafman* solos not count? It wasn't like I played notes at random—although by Professor Dorn's musical standards, maybe that would have worked in my favor. It was absurd and totally unfair!

Then I talked about it with Mr. Mackereth, who suggested

that what she probably meant was that *Deafman* was too closely tied to my practical skills, which belonged to the era in which I could hear.

She would need something new that didn't involve the guitar, and I would have to deliver.

My second idea was to score and record music on my laptop. That would surely count. So I downloaded some software and dusted off the theory I'd studied, resurrected and polished some pieces I'd submitted to Mr. Mackereth at school, and wrote something completely new to see if I still had the chops. It looked fine on the screen.

To make sure my efforts weren't completely terrible, I circulated audio files to anyone willing to listen and provide feedback.

The results were mixed.

I don't really understand anything that doesn't have a middle eight, sorry, but it sounds okay to me. Reminds me of Bach mixed with David Sylvian. (Dad)

Needs more distortion. (Sad Alan)

I like it. What's it supposed to be? (Mum)

Nice use of the Mixolydian. (Mr. Mackereth)

With a little more work, I reckon you could put EVERYONE *who listens to it to sleep.* (Roo)

Why are you asking me? Is this a trick question? (Maeve)

Yay you! (Sandra Mack—just kidding, no way did I give it to her)

I'll admit I sent in my pieces to Professor Dorn with no small feeling of trepidation. But what else could I do? Not sending them *would* be giving up, and I couldn't do that. Even though Mum and I had an agreement now, I could sense her circling, bearing a lifetime of Excel spreadsheets and soul death in her eager hands.

Would Professor D hate them and crush my dreams, or love them and save me from a life in I.T.?

Not what I expected, was her reply, the next day.

Technically good enough, but so safe. Boring, even. Who wants to be boring? I can tell your heart's not in it. Try again. Give me a reason to say yes instead of groan no. Got it?

I felt crushed. Another false victory, if you can count "technically good enough" as a victory at all. I had followed the rules and written something that wasn't wrong and wasn't awful . . . and wasn't enough. Because she was right: I had pursued a path I assumed would lead in the right direction, not one I yearned to follow.

Back to square one: feeling lost in the *woulds*. What I *would* do . . . if she *would* only . . .

G and I had talked a lot about our hopes and fears for university, but this I couldn't share with her. She had just bailed on the Judd Nelson Overdrive concert, and I wasn't entirely sure where we stood with each other. There was promise, but there was danger, too. Already, I knew she was different from the other girls I'd wanted to date. The safe ones.

The best music, like the best relationships, breaks the rules, but there are no rules on how best to do that.

I had had plenty of spare time to agonize about what it would mean if I failed Professor Dorn, since I had stopped going to deaf class entirely. Why did I need to talk to people like me when I could talk to hearing people just fine? *To* if not *with*, anyway.

The Deafman channel had become less of a time sink too. I still recorded the solos I played, but most of them I deleted now, consigning all but the ones I felt did something new to the bin —where they belonged, now that I knew they weren't going to count toward my portfolio. The remainder I posted, more or less indifferently, and my listener base suffered as a result. The one new subscriber I gained at the time was a user calling himself ThanksThroatCancer.

The name rang a bell. It belonged to a thrash band from Brisbane that had broken up years ago. I had never listened to their stuff and now never would.

Great minds wank alike, was the first message he posted. He signed it *TTC*.

Willing to be distracted from my predicament, I crossed to his account and saw that he also had a channel, ScreaMoMore. It consisted solely of screaming.

TTC was deaf too.

Well, nearly, he explained to me when I asked him about it. Down 90dB left and 85dB right, which officially counts as "profound" hearing loss. Nothing profound about it, though. Hearing aids don't do shit. Everyone wants me to get an implant. Nobody asks me what I want.

What do you want?

Well, I don't want to have my head hacked open, that's for sure. Cochlear implants sound kinda crappy, apparently. Good for speech, not much else. Why settle for second best? Go all the way or go home. That was the motto of the band, and it's my motto now.

You were the vocalist?

Yeah. Never actually had cancer, just thought the name sounded cool. Almost changed it to Thanks Chickenpox but that doesn't have the same ring. And I quit the band anyway. Too hard when I can't really hear what's going on. Still feels great to have a good yell, though. Great therapy.

Hence the channel?

Look at you—fucking "hence." Yeah, hence the channel. Gotta get it out there, the rage, the fury, the frustration. Also, my girlfriend thinks it's hot. She's Deaf too, born that way. Her implant overloads every time I crank it up. Crappy thing.

How did you learn about Deafman?

Through the mighty GlanMaster. He's into this shit. Don't know why. Have you met him?

No.

I have. Big guy from Melbourne. Got a hard-on for people who don't know when to quit. Makes him feel better about himself or something, I dunno. Hey, we should form a band! You, me, there are plenty of Deaf drummers . . . Just joshing. We'd sound fucking terrible. But WE wouldn't know, right?

I turned him down. A deaf band would definitely get publicity, but I feared it would be all in the vein of Madeleine Winter's cloying condescension. TTC wasn't offended. He had lots of other schemes.

I'm signing for a band called Manbark, for one.

Singing, really?

Not singing. SIGNing. They're real heavy, fast as shit, very political. Got a message, like a heavier version of Rage Against the Machine. I started seeing them when my hearing went—they were the best I could feel, yeah? Got to know the guys in the band. When I started sneaking in some of the younger kids from the Deaf community, the vocalist brought me aboard to get the message across properly. It's been great—and hard as hell. Like a full-on workout! If you're ever up this way, check us out.

I didn't know how to respond to that. TTC was just like me, except that he was proficient at Auslan, had a Deaf girlfriend and ties to the community . . . I didn't have a single Deaf friend; KO didn't count because it was his job to talk to me. There were barely a handful of people in the nonhearing world I knew by name, and then only from deaf class, like Hannah, our Auslan teacher, and she didn't count either. As Dad said, I wasn't a joiner.

Yeah, sure, I told TTC, knowing I almost certainly never would. He lived in a different world, one I was only visiting long enough to work out how to escape.

BLINDSIGHT

January 6

Prameela sees me waiting with G and smiles like she has no idea how badly I want my results. We both stand, and she asks us in sign how we're doing. Thumbs-up all round. Another gesture that is also a sign of the same meaning. There are surprisingly few of those. What else could we say?

G goes into the office, then emerges a moment later with a brochure, which she gives to me. I sit back down and begin to read it as she disappears again.

Neuquil Tinnitus Therapy

A grinning blond woman wears headphones that match the ones lying on the floor next to G's bed: over-ear devices like a white Bose rip-off with a long, coiled cable. Various lines squiggle around her head, representing sound or electrical waves, or both, I imagine. Subheadings reveal that I'm reading a more polished presentation of the notes Aunty Lou gave me in hospital.

This is the treatment G has been receiving. The one that hasn't worked. The one she's still continuing, if that's what she means by giving me the brochure.

I read more closely than I did the first time, willingly distracted from my own issues. G's ears are fine; her hyperactive neurons are the problem. They're like little kids, in that when they're ignored, they'll start responding to anything that even vaguely looks like it has something to do with them (Maeve had this bad when she was five). That's what causes the phantom sounds tormenting G. Those ignored neurons causing a fuss and overwhelming the working neurons that are trying to do their job.

The trick isn't to shut down the bad neurons directly, but (as with Maeve) to stop stimulating them. Ignoring them, basically, while at the same time keeping the other neurons going. By sending signals via her implant into the vagus nerve in her neck, paired with specific tones over the headphones, the auditory cortex can chill out those hyper neurons, and the tinnitus will go away.

That's what Neuquil promises. So far, though, not so good for G. But at least her neurons are still alive. All they need is the right signals to start behaving. Maybe Prameela is inputting those signals right now.

I hope so. Last night, while we lay in bed together, I traced the thin line of her newest scar, feeling for the implant in her neck but finding nothing except her pulse, a direct line to her heart.

Today, I go online to learn more. Neuquil's website is data-heavy. There are PDFs beginning with individual case studies of those who've benefited from the treatment that then go on to give details of the trials themselves. Later, I'll get Mum to look at them with me. She'll be able to interpret the stats stuffed into the fine print to see if it actually works.

Before long, I've moved on to making notes on my phone—an impossible music idea is nagging at me, and by the time G and Prameela emerge, I have a rough sketch of it down. They've been in there for ages. G looks tired (partly my fault) and emotional (understandable). Prameela walks us to the counter and, on the way, slips a note into my hand. While G sorts out the bill, I take a quick look.

> *Your results are in. They're ambiguous. I've made an appointment with you and your mother tomorrow. In the meantime, look up "blindsight." You might find it helpful.*

I start feeling tired and emotional myself. What does she mean by "ambiguous"?

G turns to me, and I put the note into the back pocket of my jeans. Prameela has gone into her office with her next patient. We are alone.

My—home—you—want—go—now?

I feel like a toddler trying to talk when I sign, particularly when I can't trust my face to say what I want it to say. I'm not even sure why I'm signing rather than using my phone. Something to do with being here, with her, under these circumstances.

Is she my deaf girlfriend?

Am I assimilating?

How long until I'm enrolled in I.T. and my life is effectively over?

G drives that question out of my head by nodding yes, and I am swamped by the greater concern for the state of my room.

I don't remember the note until after G has gone, picked up by Aunty Lou on her way home from work. G needs her headphones to continue her therapy. I can tell her tinnitus is flaring up by the way she nods along to nothing in little loops when she forgets herself. Her whole body is caught up in this condition, I am beginning to realize. Her whole world.

The first person she meets at home is Maeve, who is as smitten as I am. (At last, she texts later, a REAL girl.) The feeling is mutual. Turns out the tatty T-shirt Maeve has been wearing for weeks is merch from a roller derby team in Melbourne. They bond instantly, which gives me time to make my room presentable.

G is in the bathroom when I come back down. I quickly explain to Maeve, telling her not to be offended if G blanks out at any point.

Old news, Maeve writes on the board. *She told me while you were off hiding your porn.*

Just like that? I am faintly miffed. It took me weeks to find out, and if G had gotten her dose of the green dream right, I might never have known.

Because it mattered how I told you, she explains later, after I've introduced her to my guitars, my scary wardrobe, and some of the safer features of the room. At first it didn't matter, and then it did and I couldn't decide how, and then the easiest way was to show you rather than tell you.

Is that why you invited me to the hospital that night?

Partly. I also wanted to see you.

Why?

Because I figured you'd eventually learn to shut the hell up.

In reply, I give her a copy of my cassette, and she laughs until she pees.

Later, the lights flash and Mum comes in. I can tell she's spoken to Maeve and is thinking what I was thinking earlier—*deaf girlfriend? assimilating?*—and is slightly thwarted when I pointedly pull out my phone to talk to G and she responds in kind. Still, Mum is cool, like she's always been with the girls I've had over, and welcoming to the point where she invites G for dinner that night. But the arrangement with Aunty Lou is already made, so they raincheck for some time in the future.

The sudden permanency of this relationship is as thrilling as it is surprising, for both of us, I think. The accelerando of mutual feelings gives me as much of a rush as any music I've ever heard in my life. It seems senseless to stop and interrogate the feelings, define them, even name them—and maybe kill them in the process.

Unfortunately, time is swept up in the rush too, and I just know it's going to slam to a halt when Aunty Lou comes to collect her.

It was good to see where you create your masterpieces, Herr Sadwig, she tells me as we wait at the end of the driveway for her lift to arrive, kicking our heels on the low slate fence.

That's right, where the magic happens. Quite a privilege.

Oh, I know. Not every groupie gets to stick their nose in your bag of smelly sticks.

I told her the story about KO's deafness ritual, knowing it would get a laugh. The sachet has ended up on my bedside table by chance rather than design, and sometimes when I can't sleep, I'll pick it up, shake its contents, and see if the smell is still there. G sniffed the bag and sneezed three times in quick succession.

Less groupie, more—

Don't say "muse." That's so nineteenth century.

You mean I don't get to die of syphilis in a bordello in Rome? Things never go my way.

I lift my head and see Aunty Lou's car coming toward us. G and I stand, kiss, and part somewhat awkwardly: this we haven't yet learned to negotiate, lacking incentive. It is a minor jarring note in conclusion of an otherwise excellent twenty-four hours.

Thanks for coming with me to my appointment, she texts before I can reach the front door.

The pleasure was all mine.

That's when I remember the note from Prameela in my jeans pocket and the task she gave me: there's a word I need to look up before my appointment tomorrow. But I also have those notes on a fifth piece for Professor Dorn to get down while the details are cooperating. The more I send her, the easier it'll be for her to find three that work, right? It seems sensible to me. I hope I don't seem too desperate, even though I am.

The thought of scaring Professor Dorn away is too hot and sharp to contemplate for more than an instant, like tapping the outside of a boiling kettle.

My thoughts quickly settle on the requirements of this new work as I pass Mum and Maeve, carefully avoiding their gazes. I don't want to know what they're thinking. If I see that they're happy, I'll feel as though they're stealing what G has kindled in me, for me alone. And if they're not happy, well, screw them. I'm not ready to have this fragile bubble of positivity popped, thanks very much.

I work until midnight and even then only reluctantly send the draft description of Impossible Music #5 to Professor Dorn. This one means the most to me, assembled as it is from pieces directly plucked from my recent life. The working title is "Doom Ballet," but I fully expect that to change. Some poor student will one day write a thesis on how the great Simon Rain's creativity was stifled by his cruel professor in the earliest days of his career.

Yawning, I can't be arsed cleaning my teeth and I tug off my jeans in preparation to getting into a suddenly empty-seeming bed.

Something crackles in my pocket. Prameela's note—I forgot it again! Maybe, just maybe, I have been avoiding it.

Your results are in. They're ambiguous.

I flatten the crumpled bit of paper in one hand and Google the word she suggested I look up. The first link is to Wikipedia:

> *"Blindsight" is the ability of people who are cortically blind, due to lesions in their striate cortex, to respond to visual stimuli that they do not consciously see.*

Why would Prameela send me to an article on blindness, not deafness? I assume I've got the wrong page, but the others turn out to be about the same thing. Some blind people act as though they can see, avoiding and locating objects with uncanny accuracy, even though the parts of their brain that do the actual seeing are gone for good and . . .

. . . Oh.

Pop.

PART SIX

DEAF PERCEPTION

January 7

The mutability of the mind is both a blessing and a curse. When Selwyn Floyd raised the faint possibility that the healthy remainder of my brain might take up the burden of the part that drowned in the stroke, the idea seemed plausible—like one section of the internet accepting the traffic that a damaged section could not—and we were none of us fools for entertaining hope.

Here is proof, if I need it, of everything the specialists have told me.

Blindsight is not so much a "condition," in the negative sense, as a strange exception to what would normally be a state of complete impairment. Some people who lack all conscious ability to see a single thing are nonetheless able to navigate or make choices based on a visual sense of their surroundings. *They* are blind, but their unconscious can see and guide their actions.

These remarkable brains have not repaired themselves. The damage they have suffered merely cuts off neuronal pathways that lead to the seat of consciousness, while leaving other pathways intact. It is as though a terrorist blew up a highway while leaving various side roads intact: cars can get around the damage, even if the highway appears empty.

Do I really have an analogue of this? A new kind of sense that has yet to be discovered by science?

I can't believe I've been sitting on this knowledge all day. Literally!

I stay up late, digging deeper into the internet for answers. There's no existing term for my potential condition, not one that I can find, anyway.

"Deaf hearing," for instance, refers to a suggestion that some people learn to "feel" sound via their sense of touch, turning their entire body, effectively, into a single giant ear. I don't think that's what I have, but maybe I'm developing it?

I need to conduct more experiments. Maeve would be justifiably pissed if I started making loud noises again in the middle of the night, so instead I fish out a pair of unused headphones and start flicking through music videos at random with my eyes closed, trying to guess what the skin of my ears might be picking up. I don't "hear" anything. Whatever faint signals my skin might be detecting don't register anywhere in my brain.

Probably not that, then.

Putting "deaf hearing" aside, I turn to the general concept of what I decide to call "deaf perception." Could it be possible that the part of my brain that used to recognize sounds has been spared the ravages of the stroke? Could that part have learned to reconnect and be feeding me information about the audio world?

I have no idea how to test that theory. In bed, in the middle of the night, I am again literally in the dark. Still, I am seeing Prameela tomorrow. Cases of deaf perception might be (1) or (0), but either way she will know more than me.

I am unable to sleep. There's no response from Professor Dorn, and none from G either when I text her to see if she's up too. Desperate for distraction and impatient for any kind of response, I send "Doom Ballet" to Roo and Sad Alan, even though I know it's premature, but they're either out or asleep, and that leaves me alone in the silence of my head for the remainder of this long night's empty hours.

At 4:03 a.m., I realize that the four-month anniversary of my stroke was five days ago. That I didn't notice only makes me feel worse.

HOW I USED TO FEEL

January 8

You told us we wouldn't be miming.

Roo's response to "Doom Ballet" comes while I'm en route to the appointment. It's pretty much what I expected.

Come on. Read the notes again. You wouldn't be miming, and neither would I. We would be performing, just a bit differently from usual.

You talk as though this is a thing that'll actually happen.

It could. If Professor Dorn likes it, it might get into the undergrad concert in June, and if it does, I really want you to be part of it.

We'll look like idiots.

What're you talking about, Roo? We'll be the coolest people in the room.

Alan's support takes me by surprise. I didn't even know he was following the conversation.

All those hot music students have probably never seen anyone like us before. Metal AND kind to the disabled? We'll rock their worlds!

It would be helpful, Alan, if you stopped thinking with your dick. This isn't Slave Leia. This is Blackmod. Drip, you're asking us to stand onstage and make no noise at all. Noise is the whole point of our existence!

No, MUSIC is the whole point of our existence. Please, try to see this from my perspective. I can't do this without you.

And I can't do this sober.

All right. Two six-packs. Each.

Now you're talking.

Mum pulls into a parking lot outside Prameela's office. She asks by sign if she can come in with me. I am too tired to refuse her.

Gotta go, guys. Talk later.

Yeah, that would be good. I want to change the lyrics:

WTF, dude?

Can't, Roo. Sorry. Read the notes again.

Yeah, Roo, keep up. This is art!

I tuck my phone into a pocket as Mum and I check in with the receptionist. *Happy New Year. Is it still okay to say that? I think so. Great! Take a seat, she won't be long.* The conversation is entirely in sign, and I understand every word. Damned assimilation.

I do not want to consider the possibility that I will remain fully deaf, not now that I have a chance of being . . . something else.

• • •

"Deaf perception"? I like it. You have a way with words, Simon.

I don't care what Prameela thinks of my crappy wordplay. I just want to know what she thinks is going on inside my head!

And I reckon you're pretty much spot-on. Obviously, we can't know until I've conducted more tests—I haven't even told Selwyn yet—but it does look like we have a world first on our hands.

"What does that mean for me?"

I don't know. This may be something that's always been there, but you've only just noticed it. It may be a temporary side effect of your stroke. It may be something new that's going to improve with time.

How likely do you think that is, the last one?

Mum's question is the one I can't bring myself to voice. I stare at the screen of my phone, awaiting Prameela's answer while she gives it the consideration it deserves.

Hard to say. My instinct is that it's a very distant possibility, but I don't want to rule anything out. If I've learned one lesson from this job, it's that there's no stranger or more surprising thing than the human brain. But at the same time, it's not my job to give you unwarranted hope. It is to tell you the way the world is, as I see it. And how I see it changes depending on the information at hand—so let's get more information and see what happens, shall we?

I feel wrung out like a sponge. More information? *More*

tests is what she means. The prospect of waiting through further nights like the last one fills me with dread.

"I feel like I'm on death row," I tell them, not intending to be this honest, but the pressure inside me has to come out somehow. "Waiting for my last meal, hoping for an appeal, dreading not knowing . . . Can I hear or not? Why can't you just tell me?"

I understand.

The reply, unexpectedly, comes from Mum, who has taken the iPad from Prameela.

Or I think I do. It's so difficult to be caught between worlds, feeling powerless to do anything either way. I was like this when your father and I were splitting up. Wouldn't it be better to just finish it and move on? It was, in the end, of course—and ultimately, I did have the power to choose which world I ended up in, but for a long time I just froze, not truly realizing until afterwards that it was up to me. And you have that power too, darling. In a very different way. You are choosing, even though you don't realize it. You know, I only gave you permission to apply to study composition because I thought Professor Dorn wouldn't let you and that would help you get music out of your system so you'd learn sign language and move on. But she hasn't said no yet, and you're still trying, and I find now that I don't want you to fail, I want you to succeed, and I hope that if you just keep on doing what feels best for you, it'll work out in the end. Don't freeze. Don't regret what you never do. Don't let anyone else tell what you're supposed to be or not be—even me!

Mum takes me into her arms, weeping, and I am shocked into unexpected emotion in return. This is my mother raw and revealed, as I have never seen her before—except maybe once, the day Selwyn told her that I would never hear again. She is a woman with an ex-husband and an occasionally delinquent daughter and a difficult full-time job, and me. She is a woman who has struggled and survived. She knows something of what she speaks.

I glance up at Prameela. She is smiling. Her hands move, slowly but precisely.

Why do farts smell?

Caught by this utterly unexpected question, I shrug: *Dunno.*

So the Deaf can enjoy them too.

Back in the car, confronting the possibility of another long series of MRIs and EEGs—and who knows how many other three-letter tests—I nod when Mum signs, *Breakfast, my treat?* Ten minutes later, we're in a café ordering scrambled eggs on toast and hot chocolates, and she tricks me into talking about other people in the café.

Girl—red sweater—your three o'clock.

I look around. There's a redhead my age reading a book in one corner. I don't know her.

The only way to reply to Mum without the girl noticing is via sign.

I see—what?

Has enormous ears—like elephant.

I suppress a laugh. There's practically zero chance the poor girl can understand us—she hasn't even looked up—but I still feel shocked that Mum is doing this.

Big ears—big heart.

Says who?

Me!

This is exactly what Madeleine Winter suggested she would do if she knew sign language, but it takes my mind off everything else that's going on in the soundless bubble of my life right now. Or not going on, as the case may be. At least I.T. appears to be off the table.

Mum asks, *This week—you do what?*

That's too complicated for me to answer by sign alone.

"Wednesday there's a band I might go see with Dad, if that's okay. I wasn't going to go, but now it's a chance to test out this deaf perception thing."

Band—name—what?

"3D Owl. Some obscure electro outfit from the distant past. You know what he likes."

She rolls her eyes, which says more expressively than sign, *Do I!*

And G?

I give Mum the correct sign-name: ***George-who-loves-coffee.***

"Dunno. I haven't heard from her, which usually means her tinnitus is bad. If it drags on, I'll send Aunty Lou a text, make sure she's okay."

So then I have to avoid mentioning her suicide attempt while explaining G's home life, feeling as I do that this integrates G just a little more into my own reality. I hope that's a good thing, for both of us. The more ties there are, the harder it would be to let go, if we have to . . .

I catch myself thinking this way and wonder at myself. We're just beginning, and I'm already worried about the end!

Is she doing the same, as Aunty Lou suggested she might?

I'm not going anywhere, she said. I hold that thought so tightly I can feel it struggling for breath.

You—like—her, Mum signs. When she says "like" she performs it with her whole body, nicer than Maeve and her teasing *lo-ove* dance but still annoyingly over the top. Why can't *they* be Deaf? They'd be great at it.

"Get a life," I tell her.

Me—old, she signs. *No life.*

"What happened to Michael from the DSTO? I thought you were seeing him on Thursdays—you know, when you tell us you're out with the Pilates girls."

It's her turn to blush.

That's the trouble with living in a house full of teenagers, she says into my phone. No privacy!

"Don't tell Maeve I told you. She's holding on to it for next time she gets into trouble."

Mum laughs and taps the side of her nose. *Our secret.* I feel something alien and warm in my chest that isn't the hot chocolate, and I wonder if this is how I used to feel every day, *before*.

THE OPPOSITE OF DEAFNESS

January 15

Add birthdays to the list of things that my stroke has changed forever, along with Christmas. Music is such an intrinsic part of celebration that not being able to hear Mum and Maeve sing "Happy Birthday" made it hard to feel the requisite cheer. Silent sparklers don't seem as bright.

For my eighteenth back in October, Mum bought me a new phone, which was appreciated, given how much use I was getting out of my old one. Maeve supplied the case. For Christmas, the pattern repeated with a new laptop.

I understood: for years they'd been giving me strings, straps, pedals, picks, or whatever else seemed missing from my mountain of musical paraphernalia. It's easy to buy for someone with a clearly defined obsession. What do you do when that obsession passes and a new one doesn't immediately replace it? Going generic is much better than taking a wild swing in the dark. Unless a crack on the head is what's needed—but how do you tell that?

Dad, the slacker, gave me nothing but an IOU text on both

occasions. That's okay. He always makes good at some point. Besides, the score he gave me in September was worth two presents combined.

After I'd read it several times, back when Shari and I were still together, I asked him, **Why Mahler's Tenth? What made you choose that?**

Perhaps I shouldn't have expected a more romantic reply than Because it was on sale.

No other reason?

All right. It came with a free CD.

Seriously, Dad.

I don't know. It seemed the sort of thing you would understand better than I ever could. And less obvious than Beethoven. Like giving someone an album by the Smiths instead of Ed Sheeran. Did I get it wrong?

No, just right. Thanks heaps.

I thought that was that, but ten minutes later, out of nowhere, he sent me another text.

There really was a free CD. I haven't listened to it.

You should.

I hoped we could listen to it together one day. Do you think we still could—you with the score and me with the CD? Would that be too weird?

No, I think it'd be great. You can tell me what it sounds like.

And you can tell me what it means.

It seemed a terrific idea at the time. When we tried it, though, the day before my birthday, we lasted barely ten minutes. What Dad could appreciate in seconds just by listening took far longer to explain—and what I understood by looking at the page, I spent ages trying to capture in words. It was like trying to drive a car with your eyes shut while a passenger recited from the operating manual. A crash was inevitable.

As a prototype for the way hearing and nonhearing people might experience the same piece of music, what we did was disastrous, but as a metaphor for how life feels to me in the new year, it's perfect. A whole week flies by for the rest of the world while my life drags on without the slightest change. Still waiting for G, Professor Dorn, and results—my whole life in stasis. News on any front could fling the rag doll of my emotions in any number of directions. It's draining, trying to be ready for every possible outcome. Have I been dumped again? Has my hearing not come back? Do I have any kind of future left that matters to me?

Some of the pressure has been taken off that last question, but not all. Mum's given up on I.T. and hasn't suggested anything equally soul-destroying to replace it. Not yet. Composition has to work out, or it's back to the drawing board for both of us—just like I was with Sandra, all those weeks ago, trying to find an acceptable substitute for music.

I can think of several careers that *sound* cool, although whether they'd work for me is anyone's guess. Brewing beer, for instance. Jewelry making. Rocket scientist, even.

They all, however, require starting entirely from scratch—which, on top of learning to talk again, like everyone tells me I should do, is just too exhausting.

Roo and Alan help by filling a few of the empty hours. We go bowling, something that doesn't require language at all, really, and gives me a chance to test for any sign of deaf perception. Chest bumping, high-fiving, and giving each other the finger is the extent of our communication, beyond ordering hot dogs and beer, which I leave them to manage. I haven't been drinking much lately, because I haven't been going out much. A not entirely pleasant head spin has hold of me by the time I get home. Only then do I realize that I didn't "hear" a pin drop—not even a full strike.

At the 3D Owl concert, Dad is a willing participant in another experiment. I stand with my eyes shut, and he spins me several times. If I then correctly guess the direction of the stage, he declares it a win, and I don't tell him about the other cues I'm picking up: the movement of people around us, a general bassy vibe in the air from the speakers by the stage, and a certain inevitable amount of light leakage through my eyelids. If I was blind as well as deaf, I would still be able to point at the two decrepit band members eight times out of ten. So much for science.

Seeing KO is almost a welcome distraction from the persistent, vulture-like circling of my insecurity. He insists on peppering our conversations with signs, like he thinks I'll learn by osmosis.

Some say it's very gendered, how people respond to loss, he tells me at one point.

You know, men want to fight or fix everything, women bend instead of breaking. Me, I think that's largely rubbish, although it's true that those are two common strategies. There are others. You can view loss as a challenge to better yourself, for instance. Or as an opportunity for future gains. How? Well, the Deaf community is smaller than the hearing world, and that suits some people. If you have a phobia about loud noises, or just hate the sound of people eating—

If you think I'm ever going to agree that I'm better off this way—

Some do think that. There might be parts of you, better parts, that you would never have discovered otherwise. People, too. And places. The way you experience everything changes. YOU change. It's inevitable.

How have I changed?

I don't know you well enough to say. Maybe it's too soon, anyway. The change to your hearing happened literally overnight, but the rest will take longer. That's how it works, unfortunately. Deafness has come as a terrible shock for you, but maybe the opposite of deafness is staying the same, never changing—and that, in the long run, would be much worse.

I thought the opposite of deafness was tinnitus.

Actually, the opposite of deafness as you mean it is probably Deafhood.

Deaf what now?

He finger-spells it and follows up with a one-handed sign I don't know.

You've never heard that term? Look it up. I think you'll get a lot out of it. I certainly did.

Can you give me the one-line summary?

There isn't one. That's the point.

An activist called Paddy Ladd coined it in the nineties, he tells me. If I'm understanding Dr. Ladd's argument, Deafhood is a process or journey, a thing you're being—unlike *deafness,* the noun or *deaf,* the adjective, both of which are defined by the static fact of not hearing. Deafhood aims to capture what it's like to be deaf beyond simple hearing loss, emphasizing what's good about it, as KO suggested I could do. It empowers the Deaf, who are often victims of audism (like racism or sexism, but with hearing), to think themselves just as able as anyone else. And it encourages cooperation and communication between the many different Deaf cultures around the world—because it turns out the Deaf are not just one monolithic organization of identical clones. Of course. Losing your hearing doesn't erase every other thing that's unique about you, like being Australian, or a skate derby jammer, or a guitarist. Exactly what I was trying to tell Madeleine Winter.

I dig a little deeper after my session while I'm waiting for Maeve to pick me up.

A century or so before Paddy Ladd, George Veditz coined the

term "people of the eye" for Deaf culture—and I have a hot take on how Deafhood could actually be a thing. I mean, come on, People of the Eye! They sound like the best nu-prog band ever.

But what if you're not entirely deaf? What use is Deafhood then?

"Home, James," I tell Maeve as she comes to an abrupt halt in front of me. Maybe she screeched the tires. I can't tell.

G—where? No—see?

Her signing puts us in serious risk of a car accident. She's only been driving solo for a little while. To avoid a crash, I explain at length that I haven't heard from her and don't want to nag. The only way this works is by being patient and letting G set the terms, as her condition allows.

By giving her all the power, in other words, she dictates at my insistence.

"It's not like that."

Isn't it? Don't get me wrong, I like the girl, but if a guy tried this on me, he'd be setting the terms with his own right hand, you know what I mean?

"I know I want you to stop talking now."

Just be careful, is all I'm saying. Don't let her take you for granted, or she'll be the next one kissing footballers while sad sack Simon makes everyone's home life miserable.

She's not just right, she's also speaking to my own fears on this front, and I feel a twinge of irritation now that she's given me permission to feel annoyed—because yes, fuck it, why *am* I the one waiting around for G all the time? As long as I've known her, she's dangled me at arm's length until she's needed me, never the other way around. Is that any way to run a relationship?

But Maeve is wrong at the same time. She knows nothing about how things are inside G's head. I've only had a glimpse myself, and I'm pretty sure that not pushing too hard is respectful as well as strategic, if I want to be with her—and I do, very much. I never want that wonderful rush to stop. I have to trust her just like she trusts me and avoid burdening her with my problems. She has more than enough of her own.

Everything is fluid at my end. Who knows where I'll be next week, next month, next year? So much could change in an instant, just like it did last September. That's why all this waiting does my head in. At any moment I expect a hammer to fall.

"Don't worry," I tell both of us. "I'm not going to fuck this one up."

Famous last words. Maybe you've fucked it up already and that's why she's giving you the cold shoulder.

"Are you trying to make me miserable?"

That's my job. Little sister, remember?

She takes a corner way too fast and cuts across two lanes into heavy traffic. I hang on, imagining every other driver honking at her. Today, my deaf perception tells me nothing about that, which is probably for the best.

G

January 15

When I get home and check my email, there's a response from Professor Dorn. Finally.

To: Simon Rain

From: Grace Dorn

Date: January 15

Subject: Impossible Music

Rain—

Thanks for your patience. If you notice anything untoward in this email, it's because I am dictating. Anything to spare the hands. Software is not as good as a personal scribe, but I'm told I can't have everything.

I have been mulling over your Impossible Music proposals. There is promising material here. So promising I ran the concept past the director of the Centre for Creative Practice, using much of your original language (if writing about music is like dancing about architecture, as someone once said, then you're nimble on your feet). She thinks your technical requirements might rule you out of the undergrad concert in June—but that's no reason to despair. Quite the opposite!

The Centre just had one of their items for the Fringe Festival cancel for reasons too boring to go into here, leaving them desperately short. They know it's late notice, but they're wondering if you'd be interested in an entire program devoted to your Impossible Music idea. They have development money available, and there are fast-track disability arts grants they can access. You never know—your giant screen might be practicable! But let's dream small for the present.

There are two conditions:

(1) You need to be enrolled at the university. Fortunately, as you've convinced me that this idea has legs, that won't be an issue. Your grades are good. Your ideas are good. Consider yourself in my composition program, pending a mountain of paperwork.

(2) Enrolled or not, you're far too inexperienced to curate an entire concert, either creatively or administratively. Sorry, but that's the way it is. How would you feel about opening the concept up to other composers? I myself would be very interested in writing something for the piece you facetiously call "Miniatures/0.00005." Of course, your work will be represented. Do you have any more proposals? I like how you have incorporated graphical representation in #4 and technology in #1, but

why no dance? Seems to me that you've missed an obvious trick there.

Talk soon.

I read her email twice. The flood of conflicting emotions is just as intense the second time.

Go, *Impossible Music*! I've made it into Professor Dorn's composition course, and the relief is so great at first that I barely grasp what else she's saying. Music and me have a future after all!

A concert for the Fringe, though. That's barely two months away. It's a crazy thought—but if most of the music isn't actually heard, maybe it's not completely insane. Rehearsal schedules might not be necessary, for starters.

I look up "Centre for Creative Practice" and realize that she's talking about the Coetzee Centre, an interdisciplinary body that exists to fund things that would normally slip through the cracks of the university's creative veranda. Things like music for the deaf, it seems.

But . . . not all *my* music?

Here, my thoughts become momentarily stuck.

This was never intended to be a collaborative idea. For performance, yes, but not in conception. *Impossible Music* came out of the agony of my hearing loss and speaks directly to my experience of deafness. It's more personal than anything else I've ever conceived. How can I possibly share it with anyone?

I start writing a terse reply, telling Professor Dorn to keep her filthy claws off my idea, but in the end I never send it. Her closing sentences sink in at last, leaving me puzzled.

No dance? It doesn't seem possible that she can have overlooked the proposal for "Doom Ballet"; it is, after all, the longest of the five. And the best, in my not-so-humble opinion.

On the third reading I realize that she only mentions pieces one to four. It's almost as though she didn't receive "Doom Ballet" at all.

Could that be possible? I distinctly remember sending it.

I scroll back through my Sent folder and find it, as expected, on the seventh of January. The words in the body of the email are exactly the way I remember them.

"Doom Ballet"

Part of the thrill of loud music is the feeling of losing yourself inside it. Heavy metal is like that for lots of people. You don't have to understand a riff if it's played at high enough volume—and you can say the same about electro or even a Beethoven symphony. It blasts you into a different mental state, one in which thoughts and emotions don't really matter anymore. It's just you and whatever the music is doing to you.

The three members of local band Blackmod walk onto the stage, the first carrying an electric guitar, the second an electric bass, the third drumsticks. They take their positions on the stage. Hands at the ready. Feet too, because what the audience can't see is that the pedals that normally contribute to the sound of their instruments will actually be the instruments in this piece. Any movements these musicians make higher than their ankles will be silent.

The guitarist raises his pick. The drummer pretends to click his sticks together. The bass player chops the neck of his instrument down to begin the piece.

Projectors flare, casting light through every space in the venue—on the walls, the ceiling, the audience. The light conveys words, piercingly bright, disconnected from any obvious meaning. They come in strings that repeat in time with the pedals being activated by the musicians as they twist in a fierce parody of a normal concert. At the same time, performers move through the audience, aggressively gesturing (not signing) in a dance that encompasses hands, face, and body.

Words and movement loop around each other in knots and cascade in waves that defy any attempt to decipher them. They have clarity but no pitch or tone. They have rhythm but no timbre. They are music, and they are noise:

sounds in my head
loud
all the fucken time
screaming
fragments
over and over

earworm from hell

Look away and see shadows going berserk. There is no escaping this onslaught. It is bright. It is fast. It is unceasing:

so loud in here

hard to concentrate

can't sleep or even think

I'm so tired of this

torture

There are different kinds of deafness. Some people can hear a little, some nothing at all. Some hear too much and would kill to hear less. Like Beethoven.

24 hours a day

squeezing me out of my own head

squirting me out my ears

no room for me

driving me crazy

Because Beethoven wasn't actually deaf. He had tinnitus.

I'm fucking insane

never going to get better

shut the hell up

you have no idea

This is tinnitus for the eye.

I reread my proposal, seeing the piece in my mind playing out with incredible impact. The audience blinking and reeling from the strobe-like flashing and the flailing limbs of the dancers. Gasps from the hearing, startled signs from the Deaf. Awareness spreading that the chaotically light-filled hall is a pale echo of what it must be like to have severe tinnitus—and that there are worse things than losing something.

This is one of those works that felt like it made itself. Inspired by G, of course. They're her words, and the movements of the band evoke the cringeworthy moment when I made her cry by miming Blackmod. The "unofficial" sign language is how we first met. I'm just the guy who wrote it all down.

So why hasn't Professor Dorn even mentioned it?

Perhaps it simply never arrived. One of those internet glitches that happens sometimes. I hit Forward and start to type in her name.

G

I freeze. A list containing two contacts has appeared on the screen.

Grace Dorn

George-who-loves-coffee

Fuck shit fuck. I think I sent it to the wrong person.

"DOOM BALLET"

January 16

What to do? For starters, check that I actually did send it to G.

Any hope I have of rescue on that front is dispelled the moment I look in my Sent folder again, and there it is, in black and white.

After that point, I have no ideas.

I've been giving G space—and all my saintly patience—on the assumption that her tinnitus has been playing up, but what if that's completely wrong? What if she read the proposal for "Doom Ballet" and hated it?

Of course she hated it. I know her well enough to know *that*. I stole the words right out of her mouth, the words she shared with me in moments of great intimacy. I, who have done nothing but complain about what *I've* lost, and who just moments ago was fuming that Professor Dorn wants to steal *Impossible Music* from me, have taken from her in turn—without permission, without credit, and for all she knows, deliberately and without remorse. Maybe she thinks I actually *meant* to show her “Doom Ballet,” brazenly BCCing her in on the conversation like I’m proud of what I’ve done!

Even if she’s since guessed it was a private email sent to her by accident, what does that change? She chose her moment to tell me about her experience with utmost care. I’m planning to unveil it to the world.

It was thoughtless and selfish of me not to consult her first, before sending it to Professor Dorn.

And then, to make matters worse, I showed the guys in the band! If she finds that out as well . . . Oh, god.

I text her. I message her. I send her another email.

I just realized how badly I screwed up. I should never have written “Doom Ballet” without talking to you first. Please, let me make it up to you somehow. At least let me apologize.

No reply. I consider writing her more, but I know that badgering her will only make things worse. She’s making it very clear she doesn’t want to talk. And if her tinnitus is bad on top of that, then I’ll just be compounding the problem.

In a fever of anxiety, I contact Aunty Lou.

Is G okay? I did something stupid, and now she won’t talk to me. It would help if I knew she was all right. Hard not to worry after the last time she went quiet like this.

Thankfully, that draws an immediate response.

Is that what’s going on? George isn’t talking to me either. She’s gone out every day, but I don’t know where. I thought she was with you.

Aunty Lou's message doesn't provide the reassurance I crave. G has been going out? That's better than tunneling into the gloom of her bedroom and avoiding human contact. But where has she been going? Is she alone?

Could there be someone else?

I don't believe that. If there wasn't room for one boyfriend, there couldn't be room for another.

But what if that's the real reason there was no room for me? Maybe there was someone else all along!

I catch myself at this point. Senseless to let jealousy get the better of me. Her silence is a rebuke, and it hurts, but that's no reason to lash out in return. I hurt her first. Whatever's going on, it started with me.

Will you let me know if she says anything to you?

I can't promise that. I don't know what you did.

I understand. If you get the chance, just tell her I'm sorry.

I will. Or maybe you'll tell George yourself. You're young, both of you. Sometimes these things blow over.

I want to believe Aunty Lou, and her advice is not so different from Mum's, whom I confide in on the way to one of my many tests. Be patient, she tells me. Don't make things worse by trying too hard.

What's the difference between trying too hard and not trying hard enough?

Well, if that isn't one of the mysteries of the ages . . .

Dad is even less help, despite having a lot more experience at this than either me or Mum. Perhaps fucking up our relationships is something else we have in common.

When things break down, it's not always possible to put them back together. I mean, maybe they can be, but not every time. Don't bash your head against the wall just because you feel guilty. Walking away can be for the best, too.

We sit and watch the flashing lights in his cave, two sad dudes contemplating the ways we've fucked up.

I don't even tell the guys in the band, knowing I'll get nothing better from them. *Plenty more fish,* Roo will say. *Plenty of hot deaf fish,* Alan will add. *I only want one fish,* I'll say, and they'll give me a hard time for turning down Mia, who must surely have told them about that little adventure.

Doing one idiotic thing doesn't make you an idiot, Maeve pronounces. If she doesn't get that, then she's the idiot, not you.

I hesitate to agree, so she writes *IDIOT* on my arm, then adds *(1) Don't be an* above it. I ask her if there's a (2) and she writes, *See (1).* It sounds so simple like that. How is it that my little sister is the most help to me these days?

If G were here, she would say something like *You had one job: be a good boyfriend. That, and the coffee.*

Professor Dorn sends me a note to ask if I've thought over her email. I feel provoked by her reminder and resist the impulse to shoot back a snappy *How come it's okay for you to be slow but not me?* Particularly when she's trying to steal my idea . . .

But I know I am overreacting, and although I wouldn't tell her this, I have not given *Impossible Music* a moment's thought since I realized my mistake. Something more important has been on my mind, a realization that comes as no small surprise.

Quickly, I create a new version of "Doom Ballet," replacing every word lifted from G with random gibberish, and attach it to a reply telling Professor Dorn that I am both pleased she likes the proposals and okay with the idea of bringing in other composers. *Reconciled to* would be a more honest way of putting that last part, and it took some considerable back-and-forth between heart and head to arrive there, at a place where I could accept giving this up in order to gain something that matters to me even more. At least I know *Impossible Music* will be in good hands. Professor Dorn is well aware of where I'm coming from. Who knows what amazing take she'll have that I never thought of?

Anyway, even if my original plan was feasible, the way I feel right now, I couldn't write a lick of music if you paid me. That part of me has temporarily withered up and died in the fire of a feeling I hadn't realized until now was quite this . . . passionate.

I like G. A lot. And there doesn't seem to be anything I can do to bring her back.

Great, Professor Dorn responds almost immediately. I force myself to read on.

Great, great, great. This has to happen quickly, but I don't think that's a problem. As you say, the musical parts of the works aren't heard, so it doesn't matter if they're not perfect. Or even new. However, what corners we cut on that front would be more than compensated for by the extra design of the visuals etc., so we need to get cracking. On paper it looks achievable, though.

I'll keep you in the loop but won't burden you with the boring bits. I like doing that stuff on my own anyway. This is the fun part, before everyone else sticks their oar in.

Good for her, I think, feeling an unexpected resonance with the early days of my deafness. It was torturous and unbearable, but I did bear that torture, and I bore it alone. Life has only become complicated since I let people in.

Maybe opening up was G's mistake too. Sharing only leads to losing what little we have left.

I go into my room, dig out some old novels that do little to deflect me from my problems, and don't emerge for the whole weekend. G doesn't respond to my messages. Aunty Lou doesn't text. Maeve makes endless toasted cheese sandwiches, hoping the smell will lure me out, and slides them under my door when I stay inside. Where once I would have composed solos and deleted them, or just played them entirely in my head, I write and rewrite what I would say to G if she gave me the chance. *I get it. I'm sorry. I won't do it again. Can you forgive me?*

Eventually I stop doing even that, and just sleep.

ALL HOLE

January 19

The flash of my phone wakes me in the dead hours of the morning. I'm disoriented for a moment when I look at the screen and see that the text is from G.

Are you awake?

My hands literally shake. Do I respond or not? Maeve would advise against it, I'm sure, and part of me wants to respond with silence. It would be fitting. That's what she wants, right, to push me away before I can leave her?

But it's not what I want.

Urd. I mean yes.

What are you doing?

Nothing.

I'm at the old amphitheater by the river. At the Festival Theatre. You know the one?

Yes.

Don't take too long. It's cold out, and I'm close to convincing myself this is a dumb idea.

I'm already dressing, mentally wording a note to Mum in

case she discovers I'm gone and another to Maeve if I'm not back early and she needs the car.

On my way.

G is right. It's an unseasonably cold summer night with very few clouds, still and dark and everything you'd expect this late. The only cars apart from mine belong to cabbies and coppers, so I go easy on the accelerator. It takes all the willpower I possess.

My one detour is to get coffee from a drive-through. Two cups to go, so not just a peace offering. My thoughts need to be operating at fully caffeinated speed.

I can't fuck this up. Whether G's going to take me back or tear me a new one, she deserves me at my best.

Haven't cleaned my teeth. Wearing clothes that haven't been washed for days. Not so much as a token spray of cologne. Unwashed hair like something out of a goth crime scene.

Roo is my wingman, in absentia. He goes on dates wearing one item of clothing with a hole in it. Could be a T-shirt, his undies, the leather jacket he picked up from an op shop for a whole ten dollars. Whatever. His reasoning is that if the date doesn't go well, he can blame it on the clothes. It's not him. *He's* fine. Shame about that hole, though.

I am all hole tonight.

There are plenty of empty parking lots near the river. I slip into the first one I find and hurry across the grass, past the rotunda, to where she said she'd be waiting. The amphitheater is in shadow. I can't see her anywhere.

A panicked thought: *What if she's been attacked?* I'd be nervous, standing out here in the dark, unable to hear even the clumsiest approach.

Then another thought. Could this be an ambush? If she's enlisted the Doom Kitteh Brawlers to beat the shit out of me, I don't stand a chance.

This is ridiculous. I see her now, sitting on the highest step of the amphitheater, no more than thirty feet away. She is dressed in black jeans and hoodie, and the hood is pulled up. That's why I didn't spot her at first, despite the streetlights and starlight.

G is alone.

The screen of her phone comes on, casting a cool glow across her face. My phone buzzes.

Don't come up here, she texts. Stay where you are.

I do as I'm told, putting the coffee at my feet, opening my voice recognition app and holding it up to my mouth.

I remember seeing a show here when I was a kid. Maeve got scared and cried so much Mum had to take us home, which made me cry too. I've no idea where Dad was.

I'm talking because I'm nervous, and G isn't interested in my reminiscences.

You brought coffee?

Yup.

Bit late.

Or early, depending on whether you're looking backwards or forwards.

Downwards. Do you know why we're here?

To talk, hopefully.

Yes, but why here?

I don't know. The excellent acoustics?

Close. The excellent sightlines. You want to talk? Talk.

With that, she shuts off her phone and puts it into her pocket.

I stare at her.

What? she communicates with both eyebrows. *Go on.*

Part of me wants to run. This is too important a conversation to have while fumbling for signs and finger-spelling. What about all those speeches I prepared? Half of the words I don't know the signs for, and the ones I do I'll probably get in the wrong order!

Why?

Why not?

We stare at each other in mute resentment for a long moment. I want to sign *Sorry*, meaning for everything, but what if she misunderstands and thinks I'm sorry but I won't play her little game?

What if I won't?

She breaks the visual silence before I can.

Okay. I talk, you listen.

POSSIBLE MUSIC

January 19

I don't want to transcribe spelling mistakes and fumbles. What's to be gained by counting out the seconds while fundamental misunderstandings are painstakingly corrected? No one benefits from an accurate depiction of two people trying to communicate in a language they never wanted to learn in the first place.

This is the way we talk now. Like it or not, that's how it is. No apps. No cheats. If we can't work out this single basic thing, what's the point of talking at all?

There's no shying from anything G tells me, not if I'm to avoid failing her like I did Mum, the night I ditched Sandra. To hear G, I have to look at her. To look at her is to see her, the real her, just as she sees me signing in return, feeling every word.

Which is hard sometimes when your hair gets in the way.

But I'm getting ahead of myself.

You stole from me.

Steal in Auslan is the left hand held out flat, as though supporting an invisible object. The right hand, cupped or clawed, swoops inward toward the chest, snatching that precious object out of the air.

I'm sorry. So, so sorry.

Sorry is not enough. Tell me what you stole.

Your words. I should've asked permission.

What about the rest? My symptoms, my feelings, my fear, my anger—

I know—

I gave it to you! Not the entire world!

I know, and I really am . . . sorry.

Great, but that's not the only reason you need to apologize.

Reason is two fingers held in a scout salute to the forehead, tapped three times. I've forgotten what that sign means so she has to spell it out. This single point takes her ten times as long as it normally would to convey.

What else did I do?

You cheated on me, for a start.

What?

Don't pretend. I know all about it.

There's nothing to know! I have never cheated on anyone, ever.

Yes, you have. No matter how into someone you think you are, you've always been into music more. And music, to you, is like a girlfriend. A bad one. You gave her all your energy and attention—and now that she's cut you off, she's all you can think about. It gets fucking tiring hearing about your great lost love, let me tell you.

You're jealous? Of music?

Not jealous. Irritated. Because I may not be a great girlfriend, but at least I'm aware of my limitations. You, on the other hand, are completely oblivious to yours. I know you bent over backwards to give me space, and I appreciate that. I'm grateful for the time to sort myself out. But it's not all about me. You have to do some work on yourself as well.

Wait. I'm confused.

Confused, appropriately, is a sign that's far too confusing to describe.

About what? What I'm saying or how I'm saying it?

Both?

Grow up, Simon. Or be serious. Whatever your problem is.

All right. Why does it bug you that I love music so much?

Because you're deaf.

Lots of deaf people love music.

I know that! But they don't love it like you do. They don't turn their back on everything Deaf culture has learned and shared about their own experience of music. They just get on with enjoying it. Why are you afraid to do that? Why are you special?

I'm not afraid.

Yeah, you are. You go to concerts only with people who can hear. When you write music, you try to take it away from everyone by making it "impossible." What's wrong with enjoying what it is for you now?

Why can't someone else like it the way it used to be? It can't be so hard to break up with something that's causing you so much pain, can it?

Music is not an abusive relationship.

So prove it. Move on. Let something else in. And don't say you let me in, because look what happened. You stole from me to feed your vampire ex! It frustrates me so much that you don't see it.

I remember all those days recording solos and making *Deafman* for an audience smaller than my first gig. Were they one final fling or the actions of an addict in denial?

But what about trying to study composition with Professor Dorn? That can't be completely for nothing. I put so much into it. So much of me . . . and of her.

We'll be even if I give up music—is that what you're saying? Stop talking about it, burn all the things that remind me of it—or you'll push me away like you've pushed everyone else?

Don't put this on me. We're talking about you.

I made one mistake—

If it was just one, I'd find it easier to forgive. What about all those times you drift off, and it's obvious you're thinking about it?

I never—

That time I was in hospital? When Aunty Lou gave you my notes?

Shamefaced, I remember. That was when I came up with

the very first impossible music idea. How many other occasions have there been?

I can't change who I am, I retort with some heat, because being angry is easier than admitting that maybe she has a point.

Not all change is bad, she says. *You act like giving up music would be a negative. What if hiding behind music is the real negative? Find a way to make giving it up positive. Try saying that music is different but not impossible at all. Try possible music, for a change. Try—*

I know what you're doing. My temper fully flares now. She's sounding like Sandra channeling KO. ***You're talking about Deafhood.***

That surprises her, me knowing something about this.

Yes, I am. How did you—

I'm not a complete idiot.

Who said you're an idiot?

So what are you saying?

That things can't go on the way they were. It took me almost dying to realize that.

Anger turns to sorrow with a screech of mental brakes.

Holding a palm forward to indicate *stop*, I bring her coffee nearly to the bottom of the amphitheater steps and back away to drink my own. It's gone cold, but the hit of caffeine and sugar sorts me out a little. G comes down and squats there to drink hers. Is it a good sign that our eyes are on the same level now? Or is the second step simply more sheltered than where she was before? I can see the tops of trees swaying on the other side of the river. The desert night air is cool and bitter.

G puts down her cup so she can sign with both hands.

You never asked me why I did it. Tried to kill myself, I mean.

We are back at that precipice. I want to turn and run, but I will follow where she leads. She must have a reason for bringing this up now.

I didn't want to pry. Wasn't it your treatment failing?

Partly, but that wasn't the trigger. The trigger was you. Wait—this is not your fault. You were trying to help, and I think you did, although it didn't look like it at the time. That day we were in the university together, I started to write "Being deaf is stupid" on your phone. I stopped because deafness isn't anything. It just is what it is. And then you changed it to "Tinnitus is," and I felt this crippling mass come down on me so hard I could barely move. Tinnitus IS, I told myself, and it's never going to NOT be. Because the treatment wasn't working, and how could I possibly cope with that? Who could expect me to? After a few days of limping along, I'd had enough. I tried to explain it to you in that email I sent on Christmas Eve, so you wouldn't blame me for what I did. Mostly, though, I wanted someone to know what I was going through.

I move to go to her, recognizing the feeling of that "crippling mass," but she waves me back.

Neither of us is perfect. You're the one I'm angry with, though, so you'll just have to hear me out.

Tinnitus is what it is, like deafness. But life isn't over, as I'm proving in my own way—by going to Deaf social club to meet other Deaf people, for one. Did you ever try that?

You know I didn't.

Right. Just like you've never gone back to deaf class. You don't know what you're missing out on, because you've never actually tried. Because music won't let you. It's like . . . like you really think that if you become Deaf you'll be giving up music entirely, and it'll somehow be your fault—but the only person telling you to give up music entirely is you, Simon. You without music is like me without swearing, but I can swear just fine in sign language. Cock! Shit! Balls! See? You don't have to cut out everything you love to make room for Deafness. You just need to . . . rearrange things a little. And if you don't do that, you're going to slip through the cracks, and that WILL be your fault. You won't belong to the Deaf community, and the hearing won't accept you either. What reason will you have to live then? Taking music from people? Stealing other people's stories? Feeding the vampire? I don't think that's going to be enough. I think you'll end up exactly where I was before Christmas, if you're not already there. But if you do—if you REALLY do want that—just say, and I'm out of here. What do you WANT, Simon?

The signs for *I-want-you* and *I-love-you* are so similar that for a moment I am tongue-tied. Hand-tied. Afraid of revealing my raw underbelly, or of saying it wrong. Or of *getting* it wrong.

Maybe she understands anyway. It's her turn to look a little shamefaced.

I know, I set a bad example in the beginning, when you were actually coming to class. If we hadn't connected the way we did, maybe I would have worked all this out sooner, and maybe you would have too. But this is the way we talk now. Like it or not, that's how it is.

Is that why you went back to deaf class in secret?

Secret? It wasn't a secret. You just didn't know. And why would I tell you? You made it clear you weren't interested. You were busy doing your own thing, your Imponderable Moodswings.

She spells that out with acrimonious precision, and I feel every letter hit home.

Again, I feel a twinge of irritation. How dare she criticize me for the way I try to cope?

There's no right way to deal, G.

I know that, Simon. That's what I'm trying to tell you.

She looks down at her hands for a moment as though wondering what they're going to do next.

I—learn—sign—no—think.

Huh?

What I mean is, I'm trying to sign without thinking what I want to say in English and then translating it into

Auslan. That extra step is infuriating. I know what I want to say—why say it twice? I'm not a very patient person—

No, really.

And concentrating on avoiding English only makes the whole thing worse. I just have to keep practicing until going straight to Auslan becomes second nature. First nature, even. Do you understand that?

I think so.

I'm trying, at least, sign by sign.

So that's how I've been dealing. Making something out of the hand I've been dealt. It's a beginning, anyway. Then I'm going to get my degree and become the best Deaf counselor in Adelaide. I'm going to try skating again, when I'm absolutely sure I'm ready. I'm going to have a fucking life, not the slow, living death that I thought was all I had left. Like you think you have. I bet you've been doing nothing this week but sitting around feeling sorry for yourself—am I right?

Maybe.

It's not enough. That's really what I want to tell you. Feeling sorry for ourselves did neither of us any good.

What if sorry's all I've got?

I don't believe that. It wasn't true for me, so I know it's not true for you, either.

She's more right than she knows.

There's something I have to tell you, I sign, and my motives for doing this are unclear.

If you HAVE been cheating on me—

No, not that. But it is important, and I want you to know.

"It" is the whole deaf perception thing. How will she react to me keeping it from her? How will it affect the way she sees our future together, if she sees one at all?

Go on.

My confession is clumsy and halting, not least because I have to spell out nearly every word. There's no sign for *blindsight* or half the terms I need. It takes a small eternity to get the concept across, and even then her silence makes me wonder if I've failed.

She doesn't say anything until I've finished.

How long have you known?

I've been pacing back and forth, dreading this question.

Since the day I picked you up from the hospital. That's when it first happened. I should have told you sooner—

I'm glad you didn't. I would've hated you a little.

More than you do now?

Who says I hate you now? But misery definitely loves company. The last thing I wanted back then was to feel alone.

I'm still miserable, if it helps.

It really doesn't. Haven't you been listening to me?

Of course I have! I am. I mean . . .

I shake my hands and my head, frustrated by the need to make words with my body and think at the same time. There's a lot to be said for G's "sign-no-think" plan, I have to grudgingly admit.

I've clung to deaf perception like it's going to solve everything . . . but deep down I think I know that it won't. So what if part of my brain can maybe hear a little bit? It's not like I can or will ever hear anything again. At best, I'm a freak of nature. At worst . . . well, I'm deluding myself. That part of me—the tiny part that can maybe still hear, or even just the part that hopes I can hear—might be better off dead and buried, too. If it was, I could get on with what KO wants. And you too . . . and everyone. You all want me to be Deaf. But I don't know how to do that, not when there's this tiny bit of hope to cling to.

There are tears on my cheeks, but this admission brings no catharsis. Naming my problem now won't make it go away, any more than it did in Selwyn Floyd's office all those weeks ago.

Welcome to the club, she says. *I still hope my implant will start working like it's supposed to. Or my brain. That's my backup plan. Prameela keeps telling me that tinnitus is partly psychological, so if I feel better, my tinnitus will get better. Guess that's why I'm here. Trying to make myself feel better.*

By making me feel worse?

Yep. Is it working?

My shoulders are sore; my head hurts. It's like G and I have been physically fighting. My heart feels bruised right through.

Ugh, yes.

She says with a crooked expression, *I actually thought about never telling you. That would be the best revenge, wouldn't it? You'd be moping about, trying to get even with music for ditching you, all the while not knowing I was silently stabbing you in the back.*

Stab, stab, stab. She puts entirely too much enjoyment in acting out the blade going in. I practically feel it.

Where's the fun in that? I ask her, aiming for a measure of levity. ***You know, if this were a movie, we'd meet halfway—two semi-deaf people muddling together through a hearing world. All symbolic and shit. What do you think?***

She mimes sticking two fingers down her throat.

And something clicks in my head. A new thought, but it has the feel of an old thought that's been there for a while. Creeping up on me. Waiting for the right moment—the right phrase, perhaps, or simply the right state of mind—to pounce.

Halfway.

The problem isn't that I've lost music. The problem isn't even that I've lost my hearing.

What's killing me is that I've lost my sense of certainty.

Once, I knew what I was, who I was, and where I fit in. Then I lost my hearing, and all that stuff went with it. Playing music, being a guitarist, rocking in a band—none of those roles make sense anymore, no matter how I've tried to make them lock together. Overnight, my life went from being a model train kit with tracks stretching out ahead of me to a jigsaw puzzle with half the pieces missing.

I can't solve the original puzzle. It's never going to work. But maybe I don't have to force the pieces I have left into some ghastly mash-up of the picture on the box.

Can I find new pieces and put the puzzle together another way?

I could scream when I realize I've been doing just that. Noticing the world more effectively through my remaining senses. Learning Auslan without realizing it, to the point where I can actually communicate concepts as complicated as blindsight and deaf perception, even if it does take a while. Meeting new people who just happen to be Deaf. Catching myself feeling happy once or twice. Considering other careers, no matter how ludicrous. (Calling Dr. Rain, rocket scientist.)

This would have been unimaginable to the Simon Rain who had just lost his hearing. In fact, it's a betrayal of everything he stood for.

But, well, maybe that's okay.

Maybe the old me was too busy fighting his battles to realize that he had already lost the war.

Except that's not the right metaphor. The old me isn't gone. He's just . . . learned. Met the new Simon *halfway*.

And, as impossible as it seems, he's still me.

I wrench myself out of this sudden epiphany to pay attention to what G's signing.

You should write the script of that movie, grammar boy.

If it's a smash hit, you can give me half the royalties.

Wait—half?

You still owe me for "Doom Ballet," remember?

Are you ever going to forgive me for that?

Maybe. Ask again after the first million.

G laughs—hesitantly, but she *laughs*—and I smile hard back at her, putting all the wordless language I have into that single, silent expression.

Is this an ending or the beginning of something new?

It doesn't feel like either, exactly. I feel a bit nauseous, to be honest, and I can't tell if that's from relief or fear. The truth is still hard. Being deaf IS. But like music, it isn't a thing that's done to me. It's a thing I'm being.

That G got here ahead of me makes sense: it's easier to hide from no noise than all noise. She's had time since her second fall to fight, lose, and see the positive in giving up. That it *is* an act of *giving*, not the loss of something.

The concept is slippery in my grip, like if I ease up on it for a moment, it'll wriggle away. But I can see the shape of it now. Maybe it's something I can actually have—a future defined not by irrational demands that all things remain the same, but by the promise of change. Even if that change means new relationships with the world, with G, with music . . . *possible* music . . .

Okay, tired of being angry, G signs, hopping off the bottom step to come join me. *Intervention's over.*

Is that what this was?

Yes. How did you like it?

It sucked.

Well, it sucks not having anyone to practice with outside of classes, particularly for someone like me, who hates everyone. Almost everyone.

The sign for *everyone* is two arms held crossed at the wrists in front of the body, like a barrier, index fingers pointing in opposite directions. Open the arms to expose the body.

We are close enough to turn that sign into a hug, but I don't press my luck.

Is this you telling me I have a chance?

Maybe. Depends on what you decide to do next.

Well, for starters I'm thinking about a haircut—

Or at least washing it—but seriously, Simon!

And then I guess I'll sign up to your plan and come back to class. I can't go through this again.

It gets easier, I swear.

It better. What about giving up being a musician who's deaf and becoming a Deaf musician?

That's up to you, don't you think?

I suppose so.

G looks at me hard, like she's wondering if I'm trying to talk myself into something, or just telling her what she wants to hear.

Hear? *See*? English needs new words.

No, *I* do.

A bird flies behind her, skimming the grass and catching my eye. I look up and only then notice the lightening sky.

The pink clouds are gorgeous, so perfectly reflected in the river that the trees seem to shiver in delight. Already, it feels warmer.

So what now? I ask her.

Tell me you came in your car.

Over there, I sign, pointing through this dawn chorus for the Deaf.

She nods. *Great. You can give me a lift. And buy me coffee on the way.*

I already did that!

Consider it a down payment. Looking forward.

She puts her hands in the pockets of her hoodie—*end of conversation*—and side by side we set off into the silent sunrise.

CODA

MERELY IMPROBABLE

March 11

Elder Hall is filling fast. It's gratifying to see so many people out on such a miserable night. Heavy rain sweeps the streets in watery waves, giving everyone a flustered look as they hurry through the front doors, shedding hats and coats. The foyer smells of damp wool and wine.

I am nervous, even though this is no longer my gig. It belongs to Professor Dorn and all the other composers. Sure, four of the ten concepts are mine, and I wrote the music for three pieces plus the essay in the program booklet, but I'm a participant now, not the all-powerful progenitor.

There's no sign in Auslan for that last word. I found it in an English thesaurus.

G signs, *You good?*

Yes, I tell her because it's true. I came up with *Impossible Music* thinking it would be a way to ward off the reality of being Deaf. Now, I see it as a step along the road to a new reality—one I'm still negotiating, but at least I'm aware now that it *is* a negotiation. And it's not one I have to undertake alone.

G and I escape to our seats in the front row and sit holding hands. The buildup to the concert is a bit of a blur. Too many people and too much talking I can't understand among the other composers and their families. There's a blind woman, a young man with Downs, an old guy with one hand, and three others, each with their own story. They're all in formal dress, which makes me feel like an outsider in faded black jeans and a "Punkin" T-shirt. At least from the neck up, I look slightly respectable, because last month I got rid of my inconvenient, hard-to-maintain rock god hair. Sandra was right, again: it wasn't as big a deal as I'd feared. Now when I look in a mirror, I don't see my old me looking back.

G's hair is white now, in startling contrast with her op-shop tuxedo. Maeve pokes me hard in the back. She's sitting with Mum, KO, and Prameela, among others. My recent past is crowding in around me, but that's a good thing. It reminds me of the most important lesson I've learned in the last six months.

Dumbass that I am, it never occurred to me that hiding in my room wasn't going to help *Impossible Music* reach a Deaf audience. Those days are over, now. Everyone I've met in the community is here. I'm amazed and slightly unnerved by the turnout.

What if they hate it?

What if it all goes horribly wrong?

The air feels dense with more than just moisture, as though my preshow fears are taking on literal form. I look up at the heritage-listed ceiling and wonder if the hall has seen anything like this in its history. The Coetzee Centre calls this a world first, but that's just marketing. For me, it seems like a last chance to connect with music the way I used to. I feel a sharp pang at the thought.

Professor Dorn is suddenly in front of me, holding two thumbs up. *Okay?* She means, "Ready?"

I nod and point to the stage. *Let's do it!*

Then the lights go down. G clutches my hand again.

A spotlight comes up. Professor Dorn steps into it. Aloud, she says a few words that are repeated on the big screen behind her.

Will the hearing please refrain from using the spoken
word during this performance? Thank you.

Then a Deaf Aboriginal elder steps into the light to give a welcome in her own sign language. Auslan and English interpreters translate from the side of the stage. The glorious old woman goes off script for a while, and, smiling, the interpreters do their best to keep up.

Then they're all offstage and the lights go down for a moment.

I hold my breath, which is neither a sign nor a gesture, but is definitely part of the way we communicate with ourselves. Sitting in that illustrious hall with a small piece of the world contained tightly in my chest, I feel the puzzle of my new life piecing together at last.

Something old, something new . . .

The lights come back up, and Dad and Mr. Mackereth walk out on stage, dressed in identical black-and-white-check suits with matching bow ties. They have both shaved their heads. Their scalps shine in the lights.

Opening the concert with the piece I still privately call "Plastic Maps" was not my idea. Programming is Professor Dorn's responsibility, as was renaming every piece yet again, this time after the notes/color/mood systems devised by Scriabin and Rimsky-Korsakov. "Plastic Maps," latterly "Concerto for the Other," is now just called "C," after the key it's in. C is apparently innocence, lovesickness, earnestness, red. Minimalism triumphs once more.

The big screen lights up with a view outside. Thankfully the rain has paused, and some unwitting passersby are present to experience what will unfold.

Dad counts in Auslan: *4—3—2—1.*

Their cover of "Tokyo Go" begins.

It has been a whirlwind journey. I've written some of it down, but not all, because most of it *can't* be written down. The more Auslan I learn, the more I understand that sign language is inscribed on the water of our bodies and swept away in the moment of its creation. That makes it the best means of describing the ephemeral—emotions, lovemaking, music—and, although that makes it useless for a journal, this is in fact a positive, not a negative.

Auslan is the language of storytelling. And this is my story, with all its mess and tangles, from the beginning of the end to the end of the beginning. From deafness to Deafhood—and this new version of me I'm still getting to know.

Impossible Music may have successfully installed me in the university's music department, but how seriously will my music ever be taken? Evelyn Glennie and Professor Dorn notwithstanding, a composer who can't hear will always be a novelty, an oddity, a freak, and I'm not sure I'm prepared for that endless battle as a career choice.

On the other hand, if reading Mahler was like reading a book, why can't writing words be like writing notes?

I've decided to pursue a double major in English, so if music becomes something more like breathing than a career—an essential part of me, but not defining me—I'll have a backup plan. That crappy rom-com movie version of my relationship with G is what gave me the idea. Deafness isn't a cross to bear: it's a story. Some stories are made to be put into words, and I'm good with words, apparently. Lyrics never worked out for me before, but maybe that was because music was getting in the way.

Lyrics without music—*possible* lyrics—could be the key. What a revelation!

Funny how passion can surprise when you least expect it.

G is at uni too, of course. We spend most of our time bouncing between my place and hers, depending on who's putting what on the dinner table. I'm thinking about becoming vegetarian for the sole reason that Aunty Lou's cooking is so damned good. I concentrate on the taste when I eat rather than the absent sound of chewing: it's part of my therapy, or so I sign to Aunty Lou as I take second helpings. I've started burning some of KO's boyfriend's incense too, for the smell. For seeing and touch, I have G, which sounds creepy, though of course I like her for much more than that.

The one proposal that didn't make the program tonight is "Doom Ballet," but that's okay because it's being performed elsewhere. Privately.

One month ago, Prameela had an insight into G's Neuquil treatment. The implant forces a signal into G's nerves, a tone that is supposed to cancel out her tinnitus. But her tinnitus is not just a simple tone. They're the earworms from hell. Something a lot more powerful, therefore, is needed to cancel them out.

That's where G had the idea of reading the original text of "Doom Ballet" into a voice recorder and pumping that into her vagus nerve. *Clarity but no pitch or tone*, as my original notes said. *Rhythm but no timbre*.

Good music transforms. It's too early to tell if her tinnitus is improving or not, but she seems easier within herself now. She is here tonight, which makes me happier than I can say.

In return, I go with her to roller derby training and wait with all the other girlfriends and boyfriends. We've taught them signs to make at the other teams when ours isn't doing so well, making us a kind of hyperaggressive Auslan cheer squad.

Someone recorded us once, and we went briefly viral before the video was pulled for being obscene.

The other community I've consciously nurtured, with the help of GlanMaster, TTC, and others, is Deafman, which has become a bit of a meeting place online for musicians in my situation. There aren't many of us, but we have lots to talk about. Some are here tonight; one has come all the way from Sydney. We'll go out for a drink afterwards, the first time we'll talk face-to-face. My shyness makes mingling with strangers hard, and maybe I am too much like Dad in that regard, but through Deafman, at least, I've established things in common (beyond the simple fact of deafness) before making the difficult leap to conversation.

GlanMaster calls Deafman a dating site for sexually repressed deaf nerds. He's not so far from the truth. As another online friend says, referencing *Star Trek*: "Assimilation isn't just for the Borg."

What seems impossible alone is often, together, merely improbable.

I can't hear the applause, but that's okay. I can feel it. The program unfolds piece by piece, and soon enough it's time for another one I wrote. Now called "B♭ (rose/steel)," I'll always think of it by my original title, "A Little Light Opera."

Color organs meet modern haptic technology in the most expensive concert Adelaide has ever seen.

Just kidding!

Instead of outfitting everyone in the audience with actuator vests, gloves, VR helmets, etc., this piece relies on the people experiencing it to provide a significant part of the performance.

The concept is simple. Projected onto the screen will be a "light opera" written for a color organ operated onstage. This is the "instrumental" component of the work.

The "vocal" component is provided by performers scattered throughout the hall. Each performer responds to a particular color on the screen, initiating touch or movement that audience members will be encouraged to pass along. These messages will sweep through the hall, reinforcing and interfering with each other in unpredictable ways.

This performance is designed to unite people in a work that counteracts the isolation and loneliness frequently suffered by those cut off from "ordinary" society by deafness or other factors beyond their control.

This is an opera for everyone.

G passes a sign ("*family*") to me and I pass it on, with a grin. It worked! Sign language only feels like a straitjacket if you fight it.

The following piece is a kinetic sculpture that captures reflections off rippling water as music is fed into it from below.

The light, glittering across the ceiling and walls, is magical and strange, like someone has thrown talcum powder across a room to reveal the outline of a ghost. Music transforms, yes, but tonight music—the very *idea* of music—is itself transformed, as it has been transformed for me.

If there's no such thing as unmusical sound (as I wrote in the program guide), and if there's such a thing as musical un-sound, then *everything* is music.

"In the dark," as John Cage himself once quoted, "all cats are black."

Then it's time for me to join the rest of Blackmod backstage. Roo signs hopefully, *Beer?* But he knows the deal. He gets paid after the gig, not before. We grin and butt chests. Just like old times, one last time.

Onstage, in the heat of the spotlights, I raise my pick and await Alan's signal to begin a composition called "G."

Her face is the only one I can make out from the entire crowd.

Small word, big question.

This is how.

AUTHOR'S NOTE

To sign "thanks" in Auslan, touch the tip of your fingers to your chin, then swing your open hand forward from the elbow. For emphasis use two hands. For even more emphasis, repeat.

Imagine me making this sign most emphatically throughout what follows.

I am neither deaf nor Deaf, so how did I come to write a book about a teenage rock god who can't hear?

There are two answers to this question.

The first is that I started writing music at the age of fifteen and have dabbled on and off ever since, in the cracks between novels and short stories. Simon's belief in the musicality of all sound is mine, and his corresponding love of music is one that I feel keenly. In my early twenties, I had to choose between potential vocations—composition and creative writing—and although I have never once regretted the choice I made, I can't help but wonder where I ended up down that other trouser leg of time.

The second answer to the question of "why?" reflects my experiences with anxiety and depression arising from chronic pain in my arms and neck. Writing was the cause of that pain, to the point where giving up my career seemed the only available option. Like Simon, I endured feelings of intense powerlessness and isolation that took long periods of soul-searching to overcome. The benefits I received from reaching out for advice and support cannot be overstated.

All of this, and more, combines to make *Impossible Music* the most autobiographical novel I have written to date.

Simon is not me, however, and making him *him* took a great deal of work. This book owes a debt of thanks to everyone who helped ease his story into being.

I'll start with the members of the South Australian Deaf community that I met online and in person while working on the book. These include Debbie Kennewell, Katrina Lancaster-Maggs, and Anita Morgan of Deaf Can Do; Donovan Cresdee and Barry Priori of Sign Language Australia; Paul Bartlett; and the late Barbara Elsdon of the Royal South Australian Deaf Society. Any mistakes or misrepresentations of Deaf culture are entirely mine.

I spent several years learning Auslan, an experience that was full of challenges, surprises, and entirely new concepts. I have tried to capture the richness of sign language in these pages, but there's no substitute for getting out there and learning it for yourself. Thanks to all the teachers, interpreters, and volunteers at Auslan immersion camp—and to my classmates, especially fellow scribbler and source of constant inspiration Donna Tucker Nading, who has traveled alongside me through so much of this journey.

No mention of learning Auslan would be complete without a nod to Sarah Ann Gagliardi's glorious cakes, which sustained us through many difficult lessons.

As the book took shape, a number of insightful and obliging friends in the Deaf and hearing communities stepped up to read various drafts, including Simon Brown, Pamela Freeman, Caroline Grose, Robin Haines, Robert Hoge, Sandi Hoopman, Xander Monteath (the original "groaning ghost"), George Watt, and everyone at Jill Grinberg Literary Management. Matthew Lamb and Phil Crowley published an early version of part one in *Review of Australian Fiction*, which was valuable incentive at a critical time.

The finished novel contains contributions from family and friends, possibly without their knowledge, among them Roger Bannister, Stuart Barr, Rob Bleckly, James Bradley, Charles N. Brown (who gave me the best advice I ever ignored), Ginjer Buchanan, Chilla Bulbeck, David Cake, Zac and Naomi Coligan, Bill Congreve, Richard Curtis, Peter Dinan of Freedom Fitness, John Douglas, John Drake, Ken Evans (the world's foremost forensic synthologist), Anastasia Farley, Robin Haines, Bill and Laura Harrison of SATE Recordings, Jan Harrow, John Harwood, Justine Larbalestier, Philip Leedham, Nicholas Linke, the real and very patient Ian Mackereth (for supporting the Writers on Rafts fundraiser for victims of the 2011 Queensland floods), Chris Masters, Karen McKenna, Jo McNamara, Finn Monteath (my in-house metal detector), the late great Geoffrey Moon (who faced the difficult choice between music and painting, and chose music, much to the good fortune of his students), James Mullighan, Garth Nix, John Polglaise, Tim Powers ("Why *really?*"), Jennifer Rutherford (director of the actual John M. Coetzee Centre for Creative Practice), Anna Smaill, Gabriella Smart, Sputnik, Jonathan Strahan, Scott Westerfeld, Kathryn White, Christyna Williams, Mizzie Williams of Fisher Jefferies Barristers and Solicitors, Rachel and Sebastian Yeaman, everyone at Physio Pilates Proactive, and the members of the SF Novelist group.

Huge thanks to all of these people, and to numerous, inestimable, unbeatably gorgeous friends and family, particularly my wife, Amanda, for support through difficult times and for putting up with me talking about this book across many years (to pick just two items from a very long list).

Extra-special thanks to Anne Hoppe at Clarion Books and Jill Grinberg, the best editor/agent combo anyone could hope for, to Eva Mills and Sophie Splaff of Allen and Unwin for getting so wholeheartedly behind Simon's story, and to the incomparable Lisa Vega for her thoughtful design work.

Music and musicians play an enormous role in *Impossible Music*. Many of the imaginary examples were inspired by real people: kudos to Jason Fischer (Sproutrider), Russell Kirkpatrick (long-suffering bandmate in 3D Owl), Nicholas Linke (Punkin), Amy T. Matthews (Glam Gong), Paul Sloan (Anal

Twin, Ratsinger, übertor, The Ubiquitous Pig), and Tiffany Trent (Electric Sky Prawn's number one fan). Several enigmatic shop signs from Myanmar also proved inspirational, among them Crystal Tomato, Glan Master, Shark Venus, Transparent Art Gallery, and Triple Nine Great Integrity. One band name (Thanks Throat Cancer) came from a dream. One song title ("Peyote Squeal") came from Scrabble.

Neither the album *Depth Perception* nor guitarist Sean Williams has any connection with this novel: just one of life's excellent coincidences that he released *Depth Perception* the day I finished editing the manuscript.

Thanks to the very real Steven Wilson for his blistering track "Deafman" (via side project, the Incredible Expanding Mindfuck), for many hours of sublime music, and for speaking frankly at a Q&A in Auckland, New Zealand, about being inspired as much by books and movies as by the music of his peers. To flip the situation, I find constant inspiration in the work of musicians, so here's a big shout-out to those mentioned or alluded to in the book: Rick Astley, Avenged Sevenfold, Johann Sebastian Bach, the Beach Boys, Ludwig van Beethoven, Black Sabbath, Bring Me the Horizon, John Cage (the greatest musical genius of the twentieth century), Def Leppard, Depeche Mode, Devo, Dio, DragonForce, Bob Dylan, Evelyn Glennie, Hawkwind, "Blind Lemon" Jefferson, Jethro Tull, Jimi Hendrix, Judas Priest, Kiss, Led Zeppelin, Los Del Río, Lynyrd Skynyrd, Gustav Mahler, MC Hammer, The Meatfückers, Metallica, Wayne Newton, Gary Numan, Opeth, Orianthi,

Porcupine Tree, Rage Against the Machine, Nikolai Rimsky-Korsakov, Steve Roach, Erik Satie, Joe Satriani, Alexander Scriabin, Ed Sheeran, Slipknot, the Smiths, David Sylvian, System of a Down, TesseracT, and Frank Zappa (whose "Watermelon in Easter Hay" was a particular touchstone for many points in Simon's story).

More specifically, in the course of writing the final novel, the following albums provided inspiring accompaniment:

1i3835tra3um3, by Atom™
Hearth, by Martin Goodwin
MantraSequent, by Jeffrey Koepper
Arcadian Rhythms, by Brendon Moeller
Skeleton Keys, by Steve Roach
Earth Luminous, by Erik Wøllo and Byron Metcalfe

Thanks to each of these artists for keeping me in the groove.

A key thread in this novel is the challenge of relearning intimacy once the power of speech is gone. Among the many books written about the experience of being, becoming, or engaging with the Deaf, five provided key insights:

Islay: A Novel, by Douglas Bullard
Rebuilt: My Journey Back to the Hearing World, by Michael Chorost
Train Go Sorry: Inside a Deaf World, by Leah Hager Cohen

The Quality of Silence, by Rosamund Lupton
A Loss for Words: The Story of Deafness in a Family, by Lou Ann Walker

I encourage everyone to learn more about Deaf culture, not just by tracking down these books, but by reaching out to their local Deaf communities for opportunities to engage directly. Although my hearing has held up pretty well for someone who's listened to so much loud music, I now know that I could lead just as rich a life in utter silence as I have in the world of noise and distraction.

Researching *Impossible Music* delivered me to some other unexpected destinations. Grace Dorn's work "The Grand Kenotaphion" is based on a composition of my own that was inspired by Jonty Semper's 2CD set *Kenotaphion,* compiling a century's worth of archival recordings from Whitehall, London, on Armistice Day and Remembrance Sunday. (Other touchstone CDs include *Sounds Like Silence,* from Inke Arns and Dieter Daniels; and *From the Depth of Silence: Orchestral Music of Somei Satoh,* performed by the Janácek Philharmonic Orchestra, conducted by Petr Kotik.)

The *4′33″* app for iPhone (available from the John Cage Trust and C. F. Peters) is a glorious exultation of Cage's most famous work, one that will give you a chance to add your own performance to the repertoire, alongside mine.

Bengt Bengtsson's experiment, wearing layered headphones

in order to better appreciate loud music from a Deaf perspective, is one I experienced at the Unsound Adelaide Festival, brainchild of David Sefton, to whom eternal thanks for putting Adelaide on the international experimental music map.

I am inexpressibly grateful to the two funding bodies that assisted me at critical times during the creation of *Impossible Music*: the Australia Council for the Arts and Arts SA. This book would not have been possible without either of them.

A significant part of the first draft was written in Canberra, where I was the 2016 ACT Writer-in-Residence, an initiative of the ACT Writers Centre in collaboration with the Gorman House Arts Centre and the Museum of Australian Democracy at Old Parliament House. The manuscript was finished in Adelaide, Australia, and edited in Dublin, Ireland.

Finally, there's an international sign for Deaf pride that also doubles as "solidarity," "friendship," or even "I love you." It looks like the heavy metal devil's horns gesture, but with the thumb extended.

I am making that sign to you now.